THE

DAY NINE

R. R. Haywood

Copyright © R. R. Haywood 2013

R. R. Haywood asserts his moral right under the Copyright, Designs and Patents Act, 1988, to be identified as the author of this work.

All Rights reserved.

Disclaimer: This is a work of fiction. All characters and events, unless those clearly in the public domain, are fictitious, and any resemblance to actual persons, living, dead (or undead), is purely coincidental.

No part of this publication may be reproduced, copied, stored in a retrieval system, or transmitted, in any form or by any means, without the prior written consent of the copyright holder, nor be otherwise circulated in any form of binding or cover other than that in which it is published and without a similar condition being imposed on the subsequent purchaser

My name is Howie. I was named after my father Howard, but it became too confusing to have two Howard's, so I became Howie.
I am twenty-seven years old and before the uprising I worked as a night manager in a supermarket.
This is my account.

RR Haywood

Day Nine

Saturday

CHAPTER ONE

'Scarlett Johansson. Definitely Scarlet Johansson,' Blowers states firmly.
'She's nice but she's got a weird nose,' Cookey replies.
'Weird nose my arse, she's gorgeous.'
'Nah, I'm sticking with Angelina Jolie,' Cookey sighs.
'Only 'cos she gets her tits out on every bloody film she does,' Blowers says.
'And that's a bad thing how?' Cookey asks.
'Kiera Knightley,' Nick adds.
'Too skinny and she does the same thing in every film,' Blowers replies.
'She's a fittie,' Nick says.
'Nope, I'm sticking with Scarlet thank you very much.'
'How about you Mr Howie?'
'Me?' I reply, 'well I don't really fancy people off the telly but if I had to then it would be Monica Bellucci.'
'Who's that?' Nick asks.
'She's from The Matrix,' Blowers replies.

'Which one?' Asks Nick, leaning forward to look down the line at Blowers.
'She was the one in the toilet, telling Neo he had to kiss her like he kissed the other bird,' Blowers explains.
'Oh that one, yeah she was fit,' Nick nods in agreement, 'she gets her boobs out quite a bit too though,' he adds, 'she's been in loads of things.'
'Yeah and she's getting on a bit now too,' Cookey joins in.
'Still gorgeous though,' I add quietly.
'I wonder what they're all doing now,' Nick says.
'They're all in a secure compound with all the other fit women, being kept safe for the future of mankind,' Cookey says to sniggers from the rest of us, 'yep, they need young virile lads like us to help repopulate the planet.' More sniggers.

'Fuck the Isle of Wight then, let's go there,' Nick says wistfully.
'Oh can you imagine it...' Blowers groans.
'You can't go Blowers,' Cookey says.
'Why not...oh don't start,' Blowers groans louder this time to more sniggers from Nick and Cookey, even Clarence smiles.
'You're going to an all male compound across the road,' Cookey smirks.
'What's that smell?' I lift my head as a different odour penetrates the smug fetid stench of stale sweat, decaying bodies and farts.

'It's Blowers getting excited Sir,' Cookey says quickly.

'Burning,' Dave says. It's the first time he's spoken since we came down and rested against the wall of the old decrepit hotel lobby, waiting for the sun to come up so we can safely beat through the hordes of undead stacked up outside.

'I can smell it too,' Nick cranes his head forward sniffing at the air.

'Is it this place?' Blowers asks, 'I wouldn't put it past Smithy to set us on fire.'

'No, it's coming from somewhere else,' Clarence rumbles in his deep voice.

'Reminds me of barbeque smoke, I'm bloody starving,' Nick inhales deeply, savouring the aroma.

'Sun's almost up, we should get ready,' I climb to my feet and move stiffly over to the glass doors, peering over the heads of the deathly horde and down the hill to the now blue waters of the sea. 'Ah, another beautiful day in paradise,' I stretch and yawn at the same time, leaning against the wall as I get a sudden head rush.

'I could murder a coffee,' Clarence rumbles as he too gains his feet and stretches. I look over at the huge man and notice how he nods to Dave as he steps past him. A sign that the disagreement they had upstairs is done and finished. Dave has the sense to nod back and once again I wonder at how sometimes he can understand a subtle yet complicated social interaction but other times he misses glaringly obvious ones. Shrugging I turn back and watch as the sun's gorgeous ray's start sweeping across the pavement and each zombie instantly slows to become a shambling mess as it gets caught in the pure light of day.

'Do you think UV light would do the same to them?' I ask out-loud.

'We should try it,' Dave replies, 'they've shown they can switch between slow and fast during the day but it might work.'

'Good thinking boss,' Clarence says stepping forward to join me as I look out through the filthy glass panes of the front door. Boss? Did he just call me boss? 'If it works we could rig some up on the outside of the fort when we get back.'

'Ha, a shit load of sunbeds all hanging down from the walls, that would be cool,' Cookey laughs then looks sheepish as everyone else stays silent, 'fuck it, I thought it was funny.'

'It wasn't,' Blowers says.

'Fuck you,' Cookey pulls his bag on his back, adjusting the straps and bouncing up and down a few times to make sure everything is secure. He reaches one hand back to make sure he can grasp the stock of the shotgun. We all do the same, readying ourselves and helping each other to tighten straps, working quietly, we all know the importance of being ready to move quickly and not risk our kit dropping out. Gathering at the front door with our axes in hand, apart from Dave who still sticks with his double knives, we stand quietly waiting for something to happen.

'Er, this door is locked,' I say finally, remembering we came in through a back entrance. We all smirk sheepishly as we turn away from the door and start threading our way through the hotel ground floor. Reaching an old ballroom we find one of the double fire doors closed from the inside with a locking metal bar. Blowers gets there first and starts pushing down on it, but the bar is rusted badly and sticks in place.

'Let me try,' Cookey barges past and starts hitting down on the bar, desperate to outdo Blowers.

'Ha, yeah go on then hero,' Blowers laughs at Cookey struggling. Clarence gives him a few more seconds then coughs politely. Cookey glances round then steps back and flourishes a hand at the door.

'Watch this,' Blowers says as Clarence goes to push the bar down with one hand. Still it refuses to budge so he applies more pressure. Propping his axe against the wall he uses both of his enormous hands to ram down on the bar but still it holds. Clarence grunts with effort then suddenly stops, takes a small step back and breathes in deeply. His shoulders relax and I watch as he raises both his hands a few inches from the bar then seems to explode with a sudden ferocity sending both doors flying off the hinges to land a few feet away in the bushes outside.

'Fuck me…' Nick says in awe.
'Door's open,' Clarence rumbles bending down to lift his axe.
'Good work Clarence,' Dave says.
'Thanks Dave,' Clarence replies. Blowers and I exchange a glance at the polite tones they use to each other, both of them clearly making an effort to show respect. I raise one eyebrow and a give a little shrug before stepping out the door.
We file out and work our way through the jungle of overgrown bushes to the gravel car park. The massed horde gathered on the road at the front of the hotel start to turn slowly and shuffle in our direction.
'Righto, let's have an early scrap and go for breakfast,' I say light-heartedly.
'Or we could just skirt round them and go for breakfast now,' Nick says rubbing his stomach.
'Fuck me, look at that smoke,' we turn to stare at Blowers needlessly pointing down the hill at the thick plumes of smoke wafting up into the still morning air. Whatever it is on fire is hidden from view by the densely packed buildings.
'We've been here for one day and already things are on fire,' I remark shaking my head sadly.
'That's got to be Darren…' Blowers says quietly.
Our small group pauses for a heartbeat as we all realise the implications of what Blowers just said. As one we start jogging out of the car park, all

joking forgotten as the serious business of why we're here takes residence in our minds once more. The front of the horde have already reached the edge of the car park but we keep to the far side and skirt round them quickly. Avoiding combat now for the sake of making distance and getting down the hill. Glancing over I blanche at how many undead have gathered here during the night, the road in front of the hotel is thick with them. There must be hundreds all starting to shuffle towards us, slack jaws, red bloodshot eyes and decaying grey skin almost hanging off their bones. They look withered and less human than ever before. The tattered clothing that still clings to some of them is filthy and the blood stains have dried out to a sickening brown colour. Flies and insects buzz in and around the hundreds of raw and open wounds. The danger of disease from their dead flesh must almost be as bad as the infection inside them.
The stiffness in my legs abates as I warm up and start jogging down the hill, all of us have the sense to take it steady instead of running hell for leather. The lessons we've learnt over the last god knows how many days are what's kept us alive where many others have fallen. The muscles in my legs feel stronger, leaner and my breathing has improved with the sheer amount of exercise I've had to do since all this started. Not a day has passed without some kind of frantic run, fight, battle or chase. Blowers, Cookey and Nick also

look leaner and fitter. And despite the constant pissing about they've hardened and carry the look of capable men. I glance over at Dave running by my side, his face looks the same, the only difference is his deep tan from so many days outside in the summer sun.

Right now, at this point, I wouldn't swap or trade these men for anything in the world. There are no finer people to be with and my only regret is that we lost many such good men outside the fort.

The hill gets steeper as we descend passing old faded and battered looking Victorian town houses now converted into shitty flats with dirty windows. High gloss paint peeling from the doors and frames. The smell of burning increases and slowly we start to see the back of a huge building coming into view, smoke billowing out from the windows and roof. At the bottom of the hill we turn right to see the front of a grand old Victorian hotel blazing away. Huge flames roaring as they eat into the building. Several bodies lay scattered about on the pavement, already smoking from the heat of the fire.

'Wait here,' ditching my axe I run forward with my arm held up against the fierce heat. Reaching the first body I kick it over, but the flesh is scorched and smouldering rendering the face unrecognisable. I crouch down and crab over to the next one, rolling it over and staring down at the face, I don't recognise it so I check the next few and find them in the same state.

'Not ours,' I yell out as I reach the group, wiping the stinging sweat from my eyes. The relief is as clear on their faces as it must be on mine.

'They've got fresh bite marks on 'em, the blood is fresh too.'

'Last night then, while we were kept busy up the road,' Clarence says. I nod up at him.

'If he got our group he would have left a message,' Dave adds in his flat but firm voice, 'he'd want us to know we'd lost.'

'This whole row will go,' Nick points along the building line, at all the big old houses and store fronts joined up along the Esplanade.

'And behind too, I fucking hope there's no survivors in them,' Cookey mutters.

'There's nothing we can do, we should clear out before it attracts too much attention,' I pick my axe up and cough from the cloying stench of burning chemicals in the air. Looking back up the hill I see the thick horde slowly trailing down the hill after us. With a bit of luck they will stop and stare in wonder at the bright dancing flames.

'Which way?' Cookey steps out into the road, looking left and right.

'Up there,' Dave says quickly. He steps forward peering towards the right hand side, his eyes squinting as he examines something in the far distance. 'There's one moving away from us, going slowly,' he explains, 'he must be following Darren.' Enough said, we start jogging again. Taking a wide arc past the front of the burning building and crossing over to the far side of the tree lined pavement I stare back at the raging inferno and think of how much destruction is being wrought on the world by a few desperate survivors clinging onto life.

Our steady pace brings us closer and closer to the solitary undead limping along on a badly damaged leg. As we get closer Dave waves his arm for us to slow down and signals us to be quiet. Indicating we should follow him.

'We don't know where they went but neither does Darren,' Dave whispers as we group in close to listen, 'He'll probably go to ground and wait for us to lead him, we follow that,' he points at the limping zombie, 'and hopefully we get to him before he can do anything else.'

We're forced to walk painfully slowly as the undead struggles to shuffle on his clearly broken and mashed up leg. Going this slow gives me a chance to take in the surroundings, the debris littered about and the proper dead bodies decaying in the street. The nightclub above the bowling alley is just up ahead of us and I can see some of these dead are still dressed in their nightclubbing clothes. I think back to the young woman in the blue dress that tried to bite me back in

Boroughfare, Christ that seems like years ago but it's only been nine days.

'Do you reckon they got food in there?' Nick asks nodding towards the front of the bowling alley.

'The doors are smashed in mate,' Blowers replies quietly, 'it's already looted.'

'Might be something left, I'm starving.'

'We'll go and look mate, we're all hungry,' I motion to Nick to follow me, nodding at Dave to make sure he's okay with it first.

Nick and I sprint off to the left, leaving the group behind as we speed up and turn towards the front of the building. As we get close to the front I look back to see the others still walking slowly and then judge the distance and how long it will take them to get past us. At the pace they're going we could have a few games of ten pin and still catch them up. We drop down to a steady walk as we near the front doors and I bring my axe up to hold in both hands, watching Nick do the same. The doors are big wooden double doors, smashed and hanging from the hinges. We look down at the dried blood stains smeared across the ground and disappearing under the next set of doors. The interior doors yield as I push them open and we step gently into the slightly darker interior. Still early morning and the sun hasn't risen fully yet so the shadows in here are still long and dark.

We step slowly, going past vending and gaming machines that look dark and lifeless without electricity powering through them. In front of us is the large square reception area with rows of red and white bowling shoes stacked up in various sizes. To the left are more machines and doors leading to offices and toilets. To the right is the café, bar and restaurant which is the direction our rumbling stomachs lead us.

The bar and eating area are sectioned off by a high brown wooden wall with two swing doors, giving it a Wild West saloon look. I take point and push the doors which creak ominously as they swing open. Nick steps through behind me and they swing closed, flapping noisily a couple of times. There is a long bar to the left, seating to the right and the door leading to the kitchens is straight ahead. I nudge Nick and motion with my head towards the windows and the sight of the still limping zombie still struggling to get along outside.

We stalk towards the doorway, taking each step slowly and straining our ears to listen for any noises. A few steps away from the door it suddenly bursts open. A young Asian woman steps through quickly and stands facing us, a massive meat cleaver in her hands. Long dark hair scraped back into a pony tail frames a very pretty face, her small build stands solidly, her hands look steady as she holds the cleaver with a double grip. Eyes dart from me to Nick then back again. She takes in the big axes, the shotgun stocks poking out the top of our rucksacks but she doesn't show fear, if anything she looks more resolute.

'Hey,' I keep my tone light, 'Nick back up mate.' I step back and hear Nick shuffling a few steps away. 'Sorry, we didn't realise anyone was here, we're just looking for some food.' She stays silent, staring at Nick and then back at me.

'Those front doors aren't locked or secured, anyone could get in here.' She remains quiet, only her eyes move.

'Listen, we're not a threat to you, we came here yesterday looking for survivors from our group. A load of women and children that might have come into the harbour on boats?' She doesn't show any sign of listening, 'they might have had a few uniformed police officers with them.' Still nothing. 'That's some of our group out there,' I point out the window and watch her eyes dart over. A slight look of surprise crosses her face before she purposefully blanks it out and looks back at us.

'Okay, listen my name is Howie and this is Nick. We're from Fort Spitbank on the mainland; if you see our group will you tell them it's safe to return now?' Silence.

'Fair enough, we'll go. I don't know if you're alone or if others are with you and I don't want to know but there are hundreds of those things two minutes up that road. You need to get those doors secure.'

'Maybe she doesn't speak English Mr Howie,' her eyes flick to Nick as he speaks.

'Do you speak English? No, okay if you do understand me then try and get across the water to Fort Spitbank. It's a safe place, safer than here anyway. If you do go a big man called Chris will be there, tell him you met Howie and we're still looking for our group. Tell him Darren is over here, got it?' She doesn't respond nor move an inch.
'Come on, let's go.'
'Sir,' Nick affirms.
'Sorry to disturb you,' I say with a nod and turn my back to start walking back to the swing doors. Shaking my head at the sadness of it all.
'That's a pity, I'm bloody starving,' Nick mutters as he pushes through the doors.
'We'll find somewhere else mate.'
'Wait,' she calls out as we reach the exit door, we turn round to see her standing there holding one side of the swing door open, the meat cleaver now down at her side.
'I saw them,' she stares at us, her face still a mask.
'What?'
'I saw them come from the harbour, women and children. There were lots of them,' her voice is confident southern English.
'Where did they go?' My voice is urgent.
'That way,' she points in the same direction that the undead is slowly heading.
'Were they okay?'
'They looked okay, they didn't hang around.'

'Okay, any idea where they could have gone?' She looks puzzled for a second, 'I mean they'll go for somewhere safe that can hold that many people.'
'I don't know,' she says, shaking her head.
'Are you from here?'
'Yeah,' she nods once, still unsure.
'How many are in your group?' She bites her bottom lip and hesitates. 'Listen, I promise we're not a threat to you. We were just looking for food while we trail that zombie,' I point out to Dave and the others slowly ambling by. She steps forward to look past me through the doors and out into the road.
'Why?' She asks.
'Long story, he might lead us to someone we need to…er…' How do I explain about Darren without sounding like a nutcase?
'One of our lads got turned, he's different to the others though he can speak and think like normal. He's trying to find our group before we do. That thing might lead us to him.' Nick cuts in explaining and it doesn't sound so weird now.
She nods, seeming to understand, 'It's just me,' she says quickly, 'I mean here, it's just me.'
'Why did you come out then? This place is massive you could have hidden or something.' I ask her.
'I thought you were those things…it's daytime, they move slow in the day.'
'Didn't you hear us talking?' She shakes her head, 'And they don't always move slowly in the daytime.

The risk was too great you should have hidden until you knew what the threat was. We could have taken you and this place with ease the way you presented yourself like that.'

She stares at me defiantly and I realise the tone of voice I used was one of authority. This woman doesn't know me, who am I to tell her what to do?

'Sorry, I shouldn't have spoken to you like that,' I apologise.

'It's okay,' she mutters quietly.

'You could come with us if you want. I meant what I said about there being hundreds of those things up the road. If they get a whiff of you they'll be in here quick as anything and like I said they don't always stay slow in the day.' I make the offer but despite her poker face I can tell from spending so much time with Dave that she is worried.

'I'm Howie, this is Nick.'

'You said that already,' she replies with half a smile.

'Did I? Fair enough. What's your name?'

'Milani…Lani.'

'Nice to meet you Lani,' I nod at her.

'Is there any food here?' Nick asks. I smile at the thought that he must be starving to keep asking.

'No,' she shakes her head, 'not really anyway, some crisps and things but it all went off when the power went.'

'Crisps will do, I'm bloody starving, where are they? Can I go and get some?' Nick asks in such a friendly tone that she smiles and nods.

'In the kitchen, help yourself,' she motions behind her through the bar.

'Is that okay Mr Howie?' Nick asks before scooting off through the swing doors.

'Get some for the others but leave some for Lani here.'

'Will do,' Nick shouts.

'Lani, I meant what I said. You are welcome to come with us, you're local and we don't know anywhere round here. Some of our lads are ex-army and I guess what you're worried about but I promise no one will touch you or try anything like that.' Mentioning the thing that must be worrying her makes her react by lifting her head and staring at me defiantly again.

'I've got an idea,' I put the axe down and reach back to draw my shotgun from the bag, she steps back a little at seeing the weapon in my hands, 'don't worry, just hang on a second,' I break the gun to show the cartridges in the barrels, 'it's loaded with two shells now, this is the safety switch here. Just slide it back and pull the trigger, the range isn't good but at short range they're devastating. Here, you take it,' I hold the weapon out with the stock presented to her. She frowns at the offer and hesitates before slowly stepping forward to take the weapon and holding it awkwardly in her hands. 'Please don't point it at anyone unless you mean to shoot them, and make sure the safety is on. We

only use them when we have to; the noise draws them from bloody everywhere.'
'What about you?' She asks, nodding at the axe.
'I've got this and a pistol,' I draw the pistol from the holster in the middle of my back then realise it might be easier for her to carry that instead of the shotgun. 'You can have this instead if you want, they kick like a mule though and unless you shoot them in the head they're no good.'
'No this is fine, thank you,' her manner is instantly different, her tone less defensive now she's holding a decent weapon. Nick comes back through the swing doors, the axe wedged under his arm as he stuffs bags of crisps and peanuts into his bag.
'I got some and water too…oh…' he comes up short as Lani turns to him holding the shotgun down at her side.
'I gave it to her Nick.'
'Fair enough, do you need some shells? I've got loads,' he drops the bag and starts rummaging about before pulling out a handful of shotgun cartridges, 'do you know how to load it?' Nick asks as she takes the cartridges and starts stuffing them into the pockets of her jeans. I watch for a few seconds as Nick shows her how to break the weapon and re-load cartridges into the breach. She nods as the friendly lad chats amiably, the tension slowly easing away.
'Everything alright Mr Howie?' Dave asks, silently stepping through the door behind me.

'Fine mate, Lani this is Dave, Dave this is Lani.'
'Nice to meet you Miss,' Dave nods as though it's the most normal thing in the world to see a woman holding a shotgun in a bowling alley in the middle of a zombie apocalypse.
'Is she coming with us?' He asks in his usual blunt manner.
'I've offered mate, Lani? We could do with the local knowledge and you'll be safer with us than here on your own.'
'Yeah right, after all the scraps we've had already,' Nick laughs then cuts himself off, 'sorry I didn't mean it like that,' he adds to the young woman, 'just stand next to him and nothing will touch you,' he nods at Dave who just stares without expression, 'or the big bloke with the bald head, actually if you stand between them then you'll probably be the safest person in the entire world.' He gabbles on as she looks at him with a puzzled expression.
'Did you get any food?' Blowers asks as he and Cookey step into the foyer behind Dave.
'Why are we all here?' I turn to ask them.
'That thing is going soooo slowly Mr Howie, Clarence said he'd stay with him and we're starving, oh hello,' Blowers stops as he sees Lani and I notice Cookey gives her a big smile.
'Lani this is Blowers and Cookey, she was in here when we came in.'
'Nice meat cleaver,' Cookey smiles.

'Here,' Nick throws a bag of crisps at Cookey's head causing him to jump back laughing.
'Ah nice one mate,' Cookey exclaims. Nick throws another one to Blowers who rips the bag open and starts eating quickly.
'Is that your shotgun Mr Howie?' Blowers asks with a mouthful of food.
'Yes mate, she only had the meat cleaver.'
'Fair one, you'll need it,' Blowers says to her, 'there's shit loads of them up there,' he nods back along the way we just came.
'You coming with us?' Cookey swallows a mouthful of crisps and asks the question before stuffing another handful in his mouth.
'I…er…' she seems overwhelmed at the sight of the men suddenly in her safe place, armed to the teeth and dressed in half military gear.
'I've offered,' I explain.
'You should come with us,' Blowers says, 'it'll be nice to have someone other than this knob to talk to.' He adds as Cookey splutters with indignation. The two lads step forward and grab more crisps from Nick's bag, Cookey offers one to Lani who declines politely. Within a couple of seconds the three lads are standing round her, chatting amiably as they munch food. Their relaxed banter putting her visibly at ease.
'We'd better join Clarence before this lot eat all the food, Lani? We'd be more than happy to have you with us.'

'If that's okay,' she nods smiling for the first time.
'Of course, do you need to get anything?'
'Just my bag, it's in the kitchen,' she starts walking back through the swing doors.
'I'll come with you,' Nick and the other two start going after her, 'I'll go,' Nick says to Blowers and Cookey.
'No mate, you've done plenty of running about, just relax,' Blowers says as Cookey speeds up to go past them both. The three of them jostle through the doors following the pretty girl as I shake my head at Dave.
'Well she's got a bodyguard now,' I mutter.
'Yes Mr Howie.'
'So you and Clarence okay now?'
'Yes Mr Howie, sorry about that.'
'You don't have to apologise Dave.'
'Won't happen again,' he adds.
'It might do, just as long as we know why we're here and what we've got to do, we can all fall out as much as we like. In fact it's bound to happen but the end goal is the most important thing.' He stares at me keenly, 'What?' I ask him.
'Nothing Mr Howie,' he says flatly but holds that gaze for another second before looking away with a very small wry smile.
'Are you smiling?' I ask him, shocked at the highly unusual expression.
'Sorry, I didn't mean it Sir.'

'Don't start with the Sir stuff, what were you smiling about.'
'Just what you said, you sound like a proper officer now Mr Howie.'
'I'm not an officer Dave, I'm a supermarket manager.'
'You were a supermarket manager and you're right you're not an officer,' he accepts then looks back at me with that same keen look, 'you're a leader now and that's what officers were meant to do; lead.'
'Ah piss of Dave, fuck me mate we worked in the same supermarket.' I feel uncomfortable at the comments he makes.
'Different world Mr Howie, there's only here and now.' Thankfully we're interrupted by the return of the others coming through the swing doors and I notice Lani has a small brightly coloured rucksack on her back, too small for the shotgun to rest in so she holds it in one hand with the meat cleaver in the other.
'Dave, I found these…any good?' Blowers crouches down and rolls out a chef's knife holder full of black handled deadly looking knives. Dave is on them instantly, drawing each one out and checking the length of the blade, the sharpness, the balance and the weight. He discards most of them but leaves two long straight bladed knives similar to the ones I've seen him use so many times.

'These two are good, well done Blowers,' Dave stuffs the roll into his bag before standing up and nodding at the now grinning and proud looking lad. I head out the double doors back into the early morning air and start walking quickly towards Clarence who is still strolling slowly behind the limping zombie. I notice he keeps his eyes up, sweeping round every few seconds. He looks over at us and the new girl walking with us, smiling at her as we get closer.

'Lani this is Clarence,' I make the introduction quietly, still trying to avoid alerting the undead that we're behind him. He's well enough ahead and still shuffling along quite happily.

'Hi, you were in there?' Clarence rumbles quietly.

'Yeah,' she looks in awe at the giant man.

'You been in there since it happened?' We settle into a gentle walk, keeping a safe distance behind, each one of us sweeping round for a full view every few seconds.

'I was working in the nightclub upstairs, so is this everywhere then?'

'Yep, I watched it on television when it started in Europe and that fell in a few hours. We've been all over the south coast. London's gone, no government, no police or army, nothing.'

'I kept thinking help would come, but it just went on and on. I saw those people come on the boats and I was going to go out but I...I got scared and didn't know what to do.'

'So why confront us then?' I ask her.
'I don't know, I thought you were those things,' she shrugs as the group listen to her speaking. 'I thought they were all slow in the daytime, I've already killed a few…' her voice remains strong yet quiet as she speaks. 'Why are we following him?' She motions with the meat cleaver towards the undead trying to negotiate a high kerb. His broken leg won't lift high enough and keeps dragging him back. We stop walking for a few minutes and watch with growing frustration as he makes attempt after attempt but keeps dropping back down into the road.
'I'll go and kick him up the arse in a minute,' Blowers mutters.
'Tut tut, anything to touch an arse eh Blowers?' Cookey says quickly.
'I'm not rising to it Cookey.'
'I bet you do for him though,' Cookey says nodding towards the zombie as Nick sniggers.
'Yay….oh no…' Nick sighs as the zombie gets onto the kerb and balances for a few seconds before toppling back down again.
'They're gaining,' We turn as Dave looks back down the way we came at the mass of undead slowly shuffling into view past the now blazing buildings spreading along the road.
'Shouldn't we hide?' Lani asks in a quiet voice.

'We need to follow that thing to find out where Darren is,' Clarence replies staring back down the road.

'Darren?' Lani asks clearly confused. Blowers starts recounting the story from when they were at Salisbury barracks and were found by Dave and I. Nick and Cookey join in eagerly bragging about the exploits, journeys and battles we've had. They go quieter and more serious as they explain about how Darren got turned, how we lost McKinney and through to the final battle when we lost Tucker, Curtis and finally Jamie. Lani stays quiet throughout the whole explanation, looking to each of them in turn as they all join in with different parts. She nods and asks quick questions to clarify points and just during that short time I can see she's an intelligent person and quick to smile as the lad's infectious humour catches onto her. At the end she looks downcast and saddened, looking at them earnestly and I see both Nick and Cookey looking away as their eyes fill with tears and they swallow the sudden lumps in their throats.

'What about you?' Blowers asks, giving the other two a chance to recover for a minute. She smiles sadly as we start walking again, the zombie eventually making it up the kerb and continuing his painfully slow shuffle.

'I was working in the nightclub upstairs; I had to come down to get some change from the office in the bowling alley. It took me a few minutes to do

the alarm and get into the safe. When I got back up….it was just a mess…I thought it was just a massive fight at first but then I saw the blood and injuries, the biting and people on the floor bleeding. I ran back down and called the police but they wouldn't answer. I kept trying and trying but I couldn't get through. After a while I went back up and peeked through the door but it was even worse. I stayed downstairs after that. I could see things happening through the windows, fighting and people getting dragged onto the floor….people I knew too…I just hid there all night and most of the next day. My phone ran out of battery because I tried calling everyone but couldn't get through.'
'Have you been there the whole time?' I ask gently, she doesn't show any emotion as she speaks and reminds me of Dave the way she keeps her face expressionless.
'No, I stayed for a few days then one day I got out and went home, I don't live that far away. I kept seeing groups of those things standing about and stayed away from them, I got home but my street was full of them...so I went to other people's houses, people I knew but they were either turned into those things or just gone. I hid that night and then came back here the next day. When I got back the doors had been kicked in so I figured somebody had been in. That's why I didn't fix them, I didn't want anyone to know someone was in there,' she looks at me as she explains that bit.

'Makes sense,' I nod.
'That's it really.'
'Family?'
'No, they were in the street when I went home. They'd been bitten or whatever.'
'That's awful, I'm so sorry Lani,' I say gently, the others add comforting words too but she remains as deadpan as before.
'Mum, Dad' she shrugs, 'my little brother,' she nods as though explaining something entirely normal.
'Bloody hell mate, I don't know what to say,' I shake my head and look down at the floor, there are no words to say to someone after seeing that.
'Nothing really too say, everyone has suffered.'
'True, you've done well by the sounds of it,' she smiles at me.
'Very well,' Clarence adds with a nod at the small woman, 'so you've had contact then?'
'Contact?' She asks.
'With them, you said you'd killed a few,' he explains.
'At my friends flat, I knew he had a key hidden so I let myself in but he was already inside. He must have got bitten and got home before he turned. I stabbed him in the face, and then some more were in the corridor when I went back out.' She keeps the same flat tone, either masking her emotions extremely well or is like Dave and it simply doesn't bother her. But then she showed empathy when

the lads explained about our losses which is something Dave isn't able to do.

'Have you seen any other survivors?' I ask.

'No, none…other than the people getting off the boats but they didn't hang around. There were two older men leading them, one had a white beard.'

'The bloke with the beard was the navy captain, the other one was Ted, he was probably dressed like a policeman,' I explain.

'I couldn't see clearly but he was dressed in black and looked like he had a gun.'

'Yeah that was Ted. So any idea's where they could have gone? Where does this direction lead?'

'If you find Darren will you kill him?' She asks quickly and gets a chorus of emphatic responses from all of us.

'If you keep going along there's the esplanade and the boating lake, then it goes to a long forest area until it gets to the next village but that's a few miles away.'

'What's in between?' Dave asks.

'Couple of café's, an old tower on the beach…'

'Old tower?' Dave interrupts.

'It's really small; you couldn't fit more than a few people inside.'

'Okay, keep going,' Dave prompts her.

'The forest area, but that's got a big open space in the middle and it's not that big really, then there's Puckpool…wait,' she stops mid-stride thinking for a second, 'Puckpool is an old fort too,' she adds quickly.

'A fort?' I ask as we all stop to watch her intently.

'Yeah, it's really old, like well over a hundred years or something. There's a café and tennis court, car park but one side is really high, it's all overgrown now but there's bunkers and like underground tunnels.'

'It's worth a look, how far is it?'

'Couple of hours walk,' she stares back at me.

'Right, we can't risk leading Darren to it so we have to sort him out first, agreed?' They all nod back at me apart from Lani who bites her bottom lip again.

'Or we send a scout forward,' Dave says, 'I could go for this place Lani said.'

'We won't know where to meet, we could get separated or anything could happen, I think we should stick together.' The thought of losing Dave is almost unbearable.

'I'll find you,' Dave says confident and matter of fact.

'I don't like the idea mate.'

'How about,' Clarence cuts in, 'we go for the new place and Dave holds back to see if Darren trails us.'

'That tower is about halfway,' Lani says, 'it's a good meeting place.'

'Dave?' I look at the small serious man, he nods back in agreement. I still don't like the idea but it makes sense. We can make pace to find our group knowing our rear is covered by the most dangerous man any of us, including Clarence, has ever known. For a second I wonder if the pressure ever gets to him, if Dave ever suffers self-doubt or insecurity instead of the mammoth sense of confidence he oozes from every pore in his body.

'You won't see me, but I'll be nearby,' Dave shrugs off his rucksack and hands it to a puzzled Lani to hold. He pulls out a bottle of water and takes a long drink, downing the bottle in one long gulp, 'Lani, you take my bag, Mr Howie take my shotgun.' He hands the weapon over and checks his pistol and the two knives tucked into the back of his trousers. 'Tell me the route you're taking?' He asks Lani.

'Er, we'll keep to the beach…that's it really.'

'No deviations anywhere?' Dave asks.

'No,' she replies confidently.

'Okay, no matter what happens do not come back for me,' Dave says firmly then looks directly at Clarence, 'do not let them come back for me, wait at the tower for a while and make it so you are clearly seen going there, stay visible. Wait a few hours but if I don't come then find shelter for the night, I'll find you.'

'Got it,' Clarence nods.

'Go straight to the beach and start walking, keep the pace steady and give him time to come after you.' He nods at the lads, at Clarence and finally fixes his eyes on me.

'Mr Howie,' he nods and is gone, racing low across the road leaping over a garden wall and dropping down the other side. No noise, no crunching footsteps, just an empty void that we all feel.
'Fuck me, I almost feel sorry for Darren,' I mutter to break the silence, 'would you want Dave coming after you?'
'You'd lose,' Clarence says quietly staring at the point on the wall where Dave disappeared.
'He doesn't look much,' Lani says to shocked stares from the rest of us, but then he doesn't look much. A small quiet man and out of all of us he looks the least threatening.
'Looks are very deceiving, let's move out.'

Chapter Two

'See I told you it was a good place,' Marcy purrs as I look down from the window at the top of the four story building. She led me and my babies down the road as daylight started to hit, taking us through deserted back streets until we reached the back of one of the huge houses over-looking the esplanade and seafront. As I raced behind my raven haired zombie beauty I felt for the connection to my lovelies and knew they were with me. As the daylight hit they started to slow down but the control I have through my mind urged them to keep going and they responded with their staggering gait. That fucking Howie and his bunch of creepy weirdo's aren't the only ones that can move fast during the day.
This infection or virus, or whatever it is keeps changing. Before the big battle I had complete control over tens of thousands of them, I could feel them and see what they saw. I could make them dance, jump or do whatever I wanted. But it weakened them, pushing them too hard without food or fluids made the already dead bodies weak and I can't afford that to happen this time. That prick Howie and his little cuntrunt Dave are getting more experienced every day, so are their bum fucking little buddies.
I don't know why it changed but it feels like I have less control now, I can urge them through my mind

but I can't see through their eyes now, I can't feel what they feel and I don't know if I can tap into their collective experiences. If I'm going to be an honest super zombie then I have to admit that maybe vanity led me astray back there. I thought because of the power I had over my babies that it would be enough, but it wasn't. I should have taken my time and accessed the millions of lessons, experiences and skills my lovelies had in their undead brains.

Fuck it, fuck Howie and his fucking bunch of fucktards. This time I'm going to get strong and make my babies strong too. We'll use stealth and cunning instead of brute force. Talking of cunning, this Marcy is a cunning bitch and I can't work her out. She's gorgeous and everything a super zombie like me could wish for, but I don't know if she wants me or the power I have. Why can she talk and none of the others? Maybe the infection knows I need some help so it chose her to be the one to do it. Running through the streets I watch her bouncy backside and wish I could sink my teeth into it again, her arse tasted amazing.

Marcy led us to the back of the house and through a small car park to a single rear door. It was locked so I made one of my babies' head-butt the glass pane and reach in to unlock the door. The poor thing got the head-butt right but struggled with the concept of unlocking it and kept trying to head-butt the lock instead. I pulled it back and reached in to do it myself, groping round until I found the key on the inside and a key on the inside meant one thing…breakfast.

We could all smell them as soon as we stepped into the house. The gentle fragrance of shit mingled with piss and an over powering dose of fear thrown in.

Leaving one grumpy reluctant zombie at the door the rest of us started making our way noisily through the house. I could have made them creep quietly but by making enough noise for the survivors to hear it meant they got more frightened and released more pheromones of fear for us to follow.

Marcy and I led them through hallways and up flights of stairs, giggling and groping each other and I could tell the hunt made her excited as she kept walking faster and faster. At the top of the final flight of stairs we stopped and stared down the long corridor to the door at the far end. The stench emanating from it gave away their hiding place. Marcy started walking towards the door but I grabbed her arm and pulled her back, she spun round grinning at me as I laughed and kept hold of her.

'Please,' she begged, 'I'm so hungry,' she purred close to my ear before dropping her mouth down to my neck and starting to bite my skin. Laughing I pulled away and grabbed her wrist as she tried breaking free and running to the door. Fucking

around in the hallway I could sense the eagerness of my zombies to burst through and satisfy their craving but none of them dared to overtake me and held back, but they did groan louder and started making some lovely growling and snarling noises. That just increased the smell of the fear coming from the room ahead of us, which in turn excited us all even more. But the pleasure is in the anticipation and being the true tyrannical super zombie that I am, I made them wait until Marcy was on her knee's begging me to let them go.
'Say pretty please,' I smiled down at her frowning face.
'Pretty please,' she blinked her red bloodshot eyes up at me.
'Say pretty please oh great zombie army leader.'
'Oh pretty please oh great and wonderful amazing leader of all the zombies.'
'That's not what I said…'
'Oh come on please,' she looked up at me pleadingly, 'I'll make it worth your while,' she smiled and started rubbing her hand on my undead groin. I stayed silent for another minute or two, just so she knew who was in charge and who the boss was. But in the end the craving was threatening to overwhelm me too so I pulled her up, turned her round so she was facing the door and squeezed her behind.
'Kill 'em all,' I whispered in her ear and she was off. The sight got me going, got us all going and as a

pack we charged down the hall and ploughed into the door. It was locked from within but the combined weight of us all throwing our bodies at it soon made it crash open. And there they were, six scared little survivors. A whole family by the looks of it, old ones, middle aged ones and some young ones too.

Marcy was wonderful, leaping into them with a frenzied snarl she lashed out and sunk her teeth into one of the middle aged people who stupidly stood up to try and protect the little ones. While Marcy dealt with them I dropped down on all fours and stalked slowly towards the children, snarling and laughing. My babies were soon stuck in, chomping away amidst screams of pain and terror. Munching and slurping as blood sprayed out soaking all of us. I made them take it easy on most of the bodies and just do enough to turn them, they abided my instruction but I could sense the growing hunger in them so I let them have the little ones to eat fully. We all did. Sinking down to tear flesh open with our bare teeth and savour the hot metallic blood pumping out into our mouths. Breaking away from the feast I made my way from body to body, taking chunks out and making sure my saliva got into their bloodstream.

By the time the feasting finished the first killed were starting to come back, twitching away with convulsions before sitting up and opening their glorious bloodshot eyes. As each one came back I sensed a new connection being made and made sure they knew who I was. The more I did it the easier it got and within a few minutes I had a bigger horde. These bodies were fresh and strong, just turned and I could sense the power in them and the instant hunger they all had.

Now, standing by the window next to Marcy I stare down along the seafront and take in the sweeping bay of golden sands with the blue waters gently lapping away.

'Why are they lying down?' Marcy asks as she watches our horde all lower themselves to the floor and lay flat out facing up.

'I think they go slower during the day to conserve energy. They don't eat or drink and even with the infection doing whatever it does to us I think they still wear down and get weaker if they're pushed too hard.' Looking at them now I feel a fatherly love for them, my babies all doing as they're told and resting after a nice big meal.

'Can you connect to all of them?' She asks me quietly.

'Yep,' I nod before turning to look back out the window, 'can you feel anything with them?'

'No, I don't think so. What does it feel like?'

'Think of a bank of monitors all stacked up on a wall and each one giving a different view, that's what it was like before. I could see what they saw, thousands of them at the same time but also I could feel them too. Now the vision has gone but the

feeling is still there, like an invisible lead that runs from them to me. I could access their memories, emotions, experiences before too but that's gone now. It's difficult to explain but I can just feel them.'
'Like a telepathic connection?'
'Yeah I guess so. Whatever this thing is inside of us, it keeps changing, evolving and trying new things. It gave me so much power before but I fucked up and it feels like I'm almost being punished by having less power now. If I could tap into all the zombies and see what they saw then we'd find Howie's little piggy's and fucking destroy them. He's such a cunt that Howie. You should meet him, he's so fucking righteous and decent it makes you want to puke. And the way those little twats all look up to him, I mean who the fuck is he? Just some fucking supermarket manager, what right has he got to go slaughtering them all. This isn't some virus that's going to die out, we're a new species and we've got as much right as them to be here.'
'I do want to meet him,' she says wistfully.
'Why? Why do you want to meet him? Do you fancy him or something? Fuck me you're always talking about him, going on about Howie this and Howie that. You fucking dirty little slag.'
'I want what you want Darren, I want to hurt and destroy him for what he's done to you. I want to make him our slave, all of them our slaves and every one we turn will worship you until we've got

an army and we can sweep through this land and claim it as ours.

'Fuck me you're ambitious.'

'For you dear, just for you.'

'You're local, where would they go? Somewhere big enough to hold a few hundred of them, somewhere safe they can defend with food and water.' She stares out the window thoughtfully.

'There is a place a few miles down the beach, an old mortar battery. It's got a big café in the grounds and high walls on one side. That's the closest place that I can think of, unless they went inland.'

'No they'd stay somewhere close so that prick Howie can find his little piggy babies and take them back so they can lick his feet and tell him how wonderful he is. Fucking twat.'

'That's the first place to try then, but if they've got a few hundred people plus Howie and his men…' she pauses looking at me.

'What?' I shrug at her, 'we'll go and fuck 'em up.'

'Darren my sweetheart you're so brave and strong,' she nuzzles up to me, 'but if they've got so many and we've only got a few…'

'Then we'll get more,' I say firmly, 'we'll go house to house and find survivors and build a bigger stronger army.'

'Oh you're so clever and powerful, I wish I could think like you. Can we do it today?'

'What about hiding? We've got a brilliant view and we'll see if any of them fucktards go past.'

'Oh Darren, but you're connected to all our babies...they can rest and keep watch?'

'I know! We'll leave some here to watch and if they see Howie or his little dick friends I'll sense it, we can post sentries as we go.'

'Oh baby, it turns me on when you say such smart things,' her hand drops to my groin and starts rubbing again.

'Or we could just stay here and be the first zombies to fuck,' I say as she rubs away.

'I want that Darren I want that more than anything but you're right we should focus on getting more bodies today then we'll be safer and can have all the time together we want.' She breaks away reluctantly and I can see the longing in her eyes but I am right, we've got work to do. Time for playing later.

Leaving one of my babies at the windows front and back I gather the rest and start leading them back down through the house. As we get to the back door Marcy asks me to stop and darts off into the kitchen, coming back with two big knives she hands one to me and tucks the other in the waistband of her tight black skirt.

'I don't need a fuckin knife I'm a super zombie for fucks sake, what kind of message does that send if I have to start carrying weapons,' I say with disgust.

'It shows that you're clever and smart, it shows that you can use tools and think like normal, it separates us from them,' she nods at the gathered drooling zombies all staring at me with love and awe.

'Fuck it,' I shrug and tuck the knife into my own waistband, 'if it makes you happy.'

'You make me happy,' she smiles brilliantly and flutters her dark eyelashes at me. She is hot for a dead chick.

Outside I start leading my little horde over to the next house but Marcy says we should go away from the seafront and start a few streets back so we can avoid Howie. I tell her I'm not scared and if we see them we can fucking eat them but she flutters those eyelashes and pouts that pretty mouth and for the sake of pleasing her I change my mind and decide we should start further in the town away from the esplanade. Tactically speaking I am right, we shouldn't be near the front with so few in our group and I'm glad I had the foresight to think of moving away.

Marcy leads the way, cutting through the small streets and twisting lanes of this old town until we're absorbed in the middle of the residential area and passing huge old houses with big expensive cars burnt out on the road. We move into one wide avenue and see a small gathering of our brethren shuffling around outside a house.

'There must be survivors inside,' I remark as we stride towards them.

'Can you connect to them?' Marcy asks, pointing at the undead turning to watch us approach. I focus

hard but the only ones I feel are the zombies round me, the ones I've already bitten.
'No, just ours.'
'Try biting one of them, see if that makes a difference,' she urges me as we draw closer.
'Fuck off, you bite one of them, they're fucking filthy I might catch a disease or something.'
'Silly,' she laughs at me, 'they're infected! They won't have any diseases.'
'How do you know,' we stop nearby and watch as the new horde shuffle towards us. They might be not be connected but they still recognise a super zombie when they see one.
'Just try one,' she urges.
'No fucking way,' I shake my head. They're beautiful gorgeous lovelies all gnarled up from long days in the sun, dried skin with sunken cheeks and a lovely pale deathly pallor, but they do looking fucking gross with flies buzzing round them.
'Darren, just try it,' she pulls one forward who stares at her with a look of submissive awe. She sees my reluctance and draws her knife. Placing the sharpened edge on its bare arm she pulls the blade back slicing the flesh open and licking her lips as blood starts oozing out. 'It's different,' she feels the blood between her fingers, rubbing it between her tips and sniffing it, 'thicker and he doesn't bleed as much as a normal person would.'
'We heal faster and our blood congeals quicker, that's why they go for the either the head or a main

artery so we bleed out…don't lick it Marcy, you don't know where he's been!'

'Oh it tastes nice,' she licks at the blood on her fingers smiling at me, 'try it.'

'I'm not a cannibal Marcy, we don't eat our own.'

'Well spit in his cut then, see if that does it.'

'Oh fucking hell, come here then,' I pull his arm out and pull a big gob of spit in my mouth before letting it drool out into his freshly torn skin. As it lands Marcy rubs it in, making sure the saliva gets rubbed down and into his bloodstream.

'Anything?' She asks me.

'Nope,' I try and focus but nothing happens, no new connections or anything.

'Maybe you need your blood in him.'

'Oh well I'll just chop a fucking finger off shall I and feed it to him.'

'No baby, I like your fingers,' she purrs, 'just make a little nick in your fingertip and drip your blood in his cut.'

Shaking my head I do as she suggests, using the knife to prick the end of one finger and letting the thick drops fall into the wound. Marcy rubs it in while I close my eyes and search for any new incoming connections. Nothing happens and I smile at her, she looks disappointed for a few seconds before smiling back at me.

'Oh well, we'll just have to do it the old fashioned way my darling,' she shoves her way through the horde until she reaches the front door. Trying the handle she finds it locked but steps back to find a nice big rock to use and sends it through the glass pane. She reaches in and unlocks the door as a man comes running down the interior hallway holding a golf club above his head and screaming loudly. Marcy just stands there and waits for him to swing out, I start forward thinking she'll be hurt but she catches the golf club in mid-flight and kicks out viciously into the man's stomach. He doubles over and she drops down to rip a chunk of flesh from his neck with her teeth.

'Bite him honey,' she says to me with blood dripping down her chin. The man squirms and fights, lashing out with his fists as I advance on him. He clutches his neck and screams in anger and fear, crabbing backwards down the hallway and shouting "RUN" to whoever else is in the house. Doors open and I hear footsteps and terrified screams. Marcy is ahead of me listening with her head cocked on one side and I notice none of the horde try and push past her either.

The sense of excitement overtakes me so I swoop down and grab his ankle, lifting it up high and taking a nice big chunk out of his fat calf. He screams as I drop it and I leave him there pissing himself in fear while I charge up the stairs behind Marcy.

A woman launches herself at us from one of the upstairs room, swinging a big kitchen knife but Marcy deftly side steps and sticks her own blade

deep into the woman's stomach, laughing as she falters, trips and goes head first down the stairs.
'We'll get her in a minute…now what else do we have here…oh my…oh my oh my,' she stops in the doorway staring in. Joining her I look into the room and see a teenage male standing in the middle of the room holding a baseball bat as though ready to strike. He's a big lad, all pumped up muscles and spotty skin, clear signs of steroid abuse but he does have massively thick arms.
'Hello big boy,' she purrs and slinks a step further into the room, 'you're a big boy aren't you.'
'Come near me and I'll fuck you up,' the boy answers in a surprisingly deep voice. I lean against the door frame and watch with interest.
'I'm sure you will big boy…fuck me up that is,' Marcy draws the words out seductively, 'I just stabbed your mommy in her stomach.'
'Couldn't give a fuck, she's not my mother,' the boy answers.
'Oh step mommy is she, wow fancy a big boy like you living at home with a hot step mom like that…did you get on well?' Despite the incredible circumstances the boy's face glows red with embarrassment as Marcy claps her hands with glee.
'Oh you naughty boy…naughty naughty,' she laughs at him, 'did daddy know?'
'Fuck off,' the boy growls making Marcy laugh even more.

'I'm not laughing at you big boy, I can see why she was attracted to you with those big muscles.' Strangely I don't feel the slightest bit jealous which surprises me, new age new rules I guess.
'Did she slip in while daddy was at the golf club did she?' Marcy steps closer, keeping her hands tucked behind her back and taking small steps. She lowers her head so she can look up at him, fluttering her eyelids and swinging her gorgeous hips. He tenses up as though ready to swing but I can see his eyes are fixed on her.
'Oh Darren he's so lovely….' She turns to smile at me and I laugh with the absurdity of it, 'can I keep him? Please let me keep him,' she giggles and turns back to see him standing there looking confused.
'Tell me big boy, is it true what they say about steroids?' she slinks closer and closer to him until he could easily swing out and strike her, but he holds his pose and just watches Marcy with keen interest. She smiles at him and steps closer until she's just inches from his towering frame. 'Is it true?' she says quietly and places one hand on the groin of his tracksuit bottoms. She rubs then grips hard, 'oh it's not true…they don't shrink.' The boy grimaces with a mixed look of pleasure and confusion still holding the bat up high.
'Now listen big boy, I am going to bite you,' she keeps rubbing his groin while she whispers in his ear, 'it will only hurt a little bit and after that you'll be mine…' Amazingly he lowers the bat and stands

there with his eyes half closed. She stretches up and starts nuzzling his neck, gradually applying more pressure as her hand kneads away. Suddenly she bites down and sucks in his blood, tearing a small chunk of flesh away. He jumps backwards and clutches his neck with a shocked look on his face, staring at her then at me. I step into the room and walk slowly towards him. He backs away in fear, knocking into a desk and sending papers and mugs onto the floor.

'Take it easy, just let it happen.' I speak softly and remember how I felt when they took me down in London.

'Come on now be a big brave soldier for me,' Marcy slides over to him and starts stroking his face as his legs buckle. He falls to the floor and stares up with a look of terror and despite his size he looks young and frightened. Marcy drops down and keeps stroking his face as his breathing becomes shallower. His eyes close and we watch with interest as he gently dies right in front of us.

'Quick,' Marcy urges me and I hunker down to suck at the wound on his neck, making sure his blood and my saliva get mixed together. Drawing back we both watch intently for a few minutes until he starts convulsing, twitching and his eyes spring open to stare out with that magical bloodshot appearance.

'Welcome back big boy,' Marcy purrs and for a second I think he's about to answer but his jaw goes slack and he groans instead. The connection is there instantly in my mind and I can feel the devotion he has not just for me but for Marcy too. Two more are taken from this house and we move on, going from door to door turning those inside and gradually increasing the size of our loyal horde. With each one turned I feel the connection instantly as they open their eyes and come back from the dead.

Our pace increases as we move down the streets feasting, killing and murdering without mercy. The hunger inside all of us never gets satisfied but with each fresh kill I feel a strengthening of mind and body.

'Howie can get fucked now,' I boast to Marcy as we turn the corner into the new tree lined street with a massive following of slack jawed drooling lovelies staggering behind us.

'Yes my love, but not yet. We need more before we go after him,' she replies in a gentle tone.

'Look at these big houses with their big fucking expensive cars what good did it do them? The greedy fucking cunts with their greedy middle class jobs hiding away like pussies in their own filth and hoping someone comes to rescue them.'

'I've got an idea,' Marcy suddenly giggles, 'wait here and keep them back for a minute.' I make the horde slink into the side of the pavement and crouch down underneath a row of long bushes. They look fucking ridiculous all bending over in a long line.

Marcy spits on her hands and wipes the blood away from her face then smiles at me before sneaking forward along the garden fence of the nearest house. I peer over and watch as she goes through the gate and gets halfway to the front door before she lets out a piercing scream and starts shouting for help while she falls down to the ground clutching her leg. Within minutes I can see curtains twitching and faces looking down at the beautiful woman writhing in agony on the ground. 'Help, I've broken my ankle please help,' she screams looking about frantically. The front door opens and two men burst out racing to her aid.
'Are you bitten?' One of them asks before they get too close.
'No… I was hiding in a house down the road but I ran out of food, I panicked and started running and twisted my ankle, I think it's broken,' she groans but keeps her eyes narrowed and her hair covering her face so they don't see her eyes. I think back to the little shop on the mainland when I pretended to be a survivor. Smiling I can't help but start playing too.
'Marcy?' I call out in a strained voice, 'where are you?'
'Who's that?' One of the men asks quickly.
'It's my husband…I'm here love, I've hurt my ankle,' she cries out. I run up the road pretending to be looking for her. When I see her in the driveway of

the house I race in keeping my face down and stoop down when I get to her, examining her leg.

'Oh baby are you okay?' I ask with pretend concern trying not to laugh.

'I think it's broken,' She wails, 'these nice men were about to help me.'

'Can you help me carry her?' I call out still keeping my head down.

'Yeah but quick, get her in quick before we attract attention,' they come forward and bend down to start trying to lift her. One of them shoves his arm under her legs brushing her backside inadvertently.

'Did you just touch my wife's arse mate?' I yell at him and he recoils in alarm. 'Don't touch my wife's arse, what are you a fucking pervert? We come here asking for help and you start trying to touch her up you fucking cunt.'

'I…I didn't…' he stammers.

'He touched my tits before you got here, they both did,' Marcy shouts.

'You touched my wife's tits!?' I explode in anger.

'What the fuck?' They both stare at each other in alarm as I start laughing and hold my hand out.

'I'm only joking mate, sorry I didn't mean it but you should have seen your face…oh it was priceless.'

'What the fuck,' he repeats, 'you're fucking nuts mate.'

'Talking of faces, have you seen mine?' I stop laughing and look up at them both, showing them my red eyes and blood encrusted face. The blood visibly drains from their faces as they start inching backwards before coming to their senses and turning to run. It's too late though as Marcy and I lunge at them howling with murderous laughter. We take one each; dragging them to the ground and tearing flesh open while the house inside erupts in screams. My horde reacts quickly, pouring through the gate and entering the house with howls and snarls. Sitting back on my haunches with my eyes closed I feel my zombies as they move from room to room finding more survivors and tearing them open. I let them have their fun but not too much and I make sure none of the bodies are too badly mangled.

Fucking wonderful, this is the most fun I have ever had. Marcy and I are both laughing as we stroll through the house together so I can get my saliva into the fresh corpses before they come back.

As the day draws on the heat from the blistering sun grows hotter and our horde grows larger with every pathetic bunch of survivors we find. And with every new kill I dream of finding Howie's little piggy cunts and fucking them up.

Chapter Three

'I still haven't seen him,' Nick turns slowly round scanning the area as we walk along the concrete path at the top of the beach. The golden sands roll gently downhill to the blue waters of the sea and the lack of humanity trudging up and down with their dogs and children have left the sands unmarked and virginal. Sand blown from the beach coats the road and pathway and I guess the council would normally have maintenance vehicles out every day sucking the sand up to deposit back on the beach. Already within this short space of time the world is forgetting that humans once lived here and nature starts its gradual reclamation of what was our world.
'You won't see him,' I reply, knowing Dave and the incredible skills he has I would be amazed if he let any of us see him. 'That's him up there disguised as that lamp-post.'
'No he was behind us in that litter bin,' Blowers adds.
'I think he's kidnapped Lani without us seeing and has disguised himself as her,' Cookey says looking suspiciously at Lani, 'alright Dave?' he adds with a nod. Lani smiles and like Dave it lights her whole face up.
'I'm still bloody hungry,' Nick grumbles after a few seconds of silence.
'There's a café further up there,' Lani says.

'I wonder if they're open,' Nick says.

'Might be,' Cookey replies, 'they've got a daily special of brains on toast.'

'They used to get loads of kids down here at night getting drunk and smashing things up,' Lani explains, 'the café put metal shutters on the doors and windows so it might be okay.'

'They had gangs of kids down here?' I'm surprised that somewhere as nice as this would have those kinds of problems.

'It was awful in the summer,' Lani says, 'every kid on the Island would come over here. I used to go down here too,' she shrugs, 'nothing else to do really.'

'What about the beach?' Clarence asks.

'What about it?' Lani replies.

'There's loads to do on the beach and you've got lots of open spaces, countryside and forests.'

'So?'

'I grew up on a housing estate in London I would have killed to live somewhere like this.'

'It's pretty but boring,' she says.

'Are you from here?' Blowers cuts in.

'Thailand, my family came here when I was very young so I grew up here.'

'I love Thai food,' Nicks says clearly still thinking of his stomach, 'there was a Thai restaurant where I lived.'

'Is that the café?' I ask seeing a squat brick built building a few hundred metres ahead. As we get closer I see the shiny metallic shutters on the doors and windows just as Lani said. The café is set on a grass bank and surrounded by rows of old style beach huts and flower beds sloping down to the sandy beach. In the contrasting tranquil beauty of the area the shutters look ugly and urban, a sign that all was not well in the life we thought was civil and ordered.

'The towers just there,' Lani points further up the beach to a Disney looking structure; a small single castle tower looking distinctly out of place.

'Right I'm bloody famished, we'll get in that café and get some proper food. Cookey and Blowers go round the back and see if you can find a way in. Nick you watch the way we came from, Clarence you okay watching ahead?'

'Yes boss,' Clarence replies striding a few steps forward to get a good view. Cookey and Blowers quickly peel off as Nick walks back a few steps and turns to watch the route we just took, leaving Lani and I standing together.

'So you were in the army then?' Lani asks after a few seconds.

'Me? No I was a night manager in a supermarket. I worked with Dave; he was in the army a few years ago, Clarence too.'

'Oh I thought you were. You look like you were in the army.'

'Do I?' I laugh quietly, 'I guess that's better than looking like a supermarket manager.'

'But you're in charge of them all?' She asks with a serious look.

'Well…kind of I guess that just sort of happened on its own. It's weird really, how it came about. I was desperate to get to London to find my sister and things kept happening that slowed me down so I just kind of took over so I could do what I needed to get done…if that makes any sense at all,' I shake my head smiling wryly at the memories of the last nine days.

'Your sister? She's with the group that came here?'

'Yeah, they've got some good people with them so they should be okay.'

'Mr Howie, the rear doors are shuttered too. We'll need a vehicle or something to pull them off,' Blowers calls out as he and Cookey appear from the side of the building.

'Nick! Can you hotwire a car mate?' I call out.

'Older ones are easier than new ones Mr Howie, I've never done one but it can't be that hard.'

'Nick is brilliant with electrical things,' I say to Lani, 'he hotwired Tower Bridge in London a few days ago.'

'We just need a car now,' Blowers says joining us with Cookey.

'There's a car park up there,' Lani points up the hill behind the café.

'Is it open land or are there places for those things to hide?' I ask her.

'It's all open, literally like a two minute walk. I'll go with Nick if you want and show him.'
'Take Blowers with you, Cookey you go a bit further up and keep a line of sight with them and us, I'll take Nick's position.' They move off as I take over, watching the rear while Clarence stands solidly watching ahead and scanning round every few seconds. The beach is on my right with the pavement and then the road ahead of me. On the left is a high old stone built wall with huge tree branches hanging low. Dave must be behind that wall somewhere, he could be there now watching me. I give a little wave in case he is watching, then feeling stupid I stick one finger up and smile to myself hoping he's not offended. But then I don't think it is even possible to offend Dave, apart from that time I broke his shotgun in Portsmouth. I wonder how Chris is getting on, if he's got our fort back up and running yet. It's funny but already I'm thinking of it as sort of home, the place where we need to get back to. There's no rules now, no society that demands we act or behave in a certain way. Any one of these lads or Clarence could just say fuck it and walk off to live how they want. But we all know we're stronger together and there is an incredible bond between us already.
Lani's words replay in my head, that I'm the one in charge. I don't mean to boss them about but it just feels natural now and even with Clarence and Dave I can feel them waiting and watching for the

decisions to come from me. Even when I defer to their skills and experiences it's just a given that it will be me making the final decision. People are strange, the need to have that pecking order even when the world is ending. There could be hundreds or thousands of groups like ours with normal everyday people that had mundane jobs suddenly thrust forward and taking leadership.
The sounds of smashing glass followed by vehicle alarms rings out for a few seconds and I imagine Nick quickly releasing the bonnet clasps to detach the battery wires. The sounds cut off as expected and are followed a few minutes later by an engine roaring to life. I listen as the sound draws closer until an old red van comes into view bouncing over the grass and slewing round the side of the café with a grinning Nick at the wheel and Lani sitting next to him laughing. Blowers and Cookey come jogging behind it with Blowers yelling abuse at Nick for making them both run. The van comes to a halt and Nick gets out laughing and pointing at Blowers, Lani clambers down holding a thick tow rope coiled over one shoulder.
The lads piss about as they hook one end onto the shutters and fasten the other end to the van. Between them they work quickly and in good humour and I watch Lani joining in laughing and joking with them. With a gesture from Blowers she jogs forward and climbs into the driver's seat and again I wonder at the pecking order of human life.

Even amongst those few young people Blowers assumes the role of leader and directs the others. They laugh and joke but even so, they do as instructed and without question.

'Now Lani!' Blowers shouts. The van surges forward with Lani at the wheel, the rope goes instantly taut and rips the shutters from the frame with a loud wrenching noise followed by a metallic clang as it bounces on the concrete ground. Nick and Cookey get to the door together and start synchronised kicks until the thick wooden door bursts open. They all cheer at the small victory and I watch with interest as they all instinctively turn to look at me, waiting for my response and the next instruction.

'Brilliant! Well done, me and Clarence will stay here while you get some food, Lani make sure they don't eat anything poisonous,' she laughs and nods as they disappear into the café. Looking up I see Clarence smiling at me with a huge grin and I stroll over to him, making sure I've got a good view of the surrounding area.

'She seems nice,' I remark to the big man.

He nods back, 'been through it by what she says,' he replies.

'I worry though mate, we've got this far thanks to Dave and you but what if something happens and we lose him, or lose you...'

'You'll survive as long as you stay together.'

'Yeah maybe but we need to increase our chances, mate maybe you and Dave could give us some training or something. Not just in guns but with other weapons like knives or something.'

'I've seen you fight,' Clarence grins, 'I've watched all of you fight, it's wild but it's brutal and it works. Training could confuse or restrain what you're doing naturally.'

'Okay…just a thought.'

'What are they doing?'

Looking over I watch Nick and Cookey dragging a large wooden table down onto the middle of the path followed by Blowers carrying handfuls of drinks and food. Nick and Cookey go back inside and come back out within seconds carrying more grub until the table is laden with packets, bags and bottles of water and juice. Lani appears carrying a big bowl of fruit.

'Fruit!' Clarence smiles and starts walking towards her, 'any bananas?' he calls out.

'They're mouldy and black,' Lani replies 'but there's some apples and oranges here.'

'Dave said to wait at the tower but I guess this is close enough, just make sure we keep a good watch,' I sit down at the table and select a big green apple, looking at it closely before I sink my teeth into it and feel the fresh juice burst into my mouth. 'Oh that's so good.'

'There's a barbeque inside with a gas bottle, I've got it going to make hot water for coffee,' Nick comes out smiling and rubbing his hands together. A few minutes later I'm watching as the lads devour everything in front of them while Lani eats politely. I can see she's hungry but she restrains herself from going mad, unlike the rest of us who go at it like crazy.

Sitting in the beautiful warm sunlight we could almost forget why we're here and what we're here for. The food gets eaten and Nick goes back into the café with Lani before re-appearing a few minutes later with a tray of plain white coffee mugs all steaming away.

'Milk portions!' Cookey exclaims, delighted at the sight of the individual long life milk sachets. He rips the top off one and drinks it down quickly.

'Oh look at this,' Blowers groans with pleasure, 'coffee, sugar and milk…' like I said, small victories make for the best feelings sometimes and for this short amount of time while the world crumbles around us and with a town full of cannibal zombies ready to rip our hearts out, we sit in the sun drinking coffee. Nick breaks out a packet of cigarettes and hands them round, Blowers, Cookey and Lani take one each and are soon sitting there in a state of bliss. The temptation is too much so I slide one out of the packet and light it up, inhaling deeply I hold the smoke in my lungs for a second before blowing it out gently and immediately doubling over with a coughing fit.

'Shit, I haven't had one for ages,' I wipe the tears from my eyes and take another drag as the others laugh at my sorry state.
'You shouldn't smoke Mr Howie,' Dave's voice surprises us all, making us jump and start going for weapons laying within grabbing reach. He's leaning against the corner of the café watching us benignly.
'How long have you been there?' I splutter.
'Only a second or two,' he walks over and sits down next to Clarence. Taking a bottle of water he screws the top off before downing it in one.
'I'll get you a coffee Dave,' Nick gets up heading towards the café.
'Is there herbal tea?' Dave asks into a sudden silence as we all take in what he just asked for.
'Herbal tea?' Nick asks.
'Camomile or Peppermint,' Dave says. Taking an apple from the nearly empty bowl, he pulls a small knife from a pocket and starts cutting chunks off.
'Right...yeah...I'll er have a look,' Nick says. Dave puts the chunk of apple in his mouth before looking up and seeing us all staring at him.
'I like herbal tea,' he shrugs and cuts another chunk of apple.
'Fair enough mate, did you see anything?' I ask him.
'Nothing,' he shakes his head and looks at me, 'something isn't right, I can feel it. There's no movement, nothing was following you...nothing,' he adds.

'That's a good thing right?' Cookey asks.
'Should be,' Dave replies, 'but it isn't…'
'Why not?' Blowers cuts in.
'It means Darren has found something else to do,' Clarence says, 'something more important than coming after us.'
'I see,' I reply, 'what could that be? If I was him I would be trying to build resources again, getting more of those things before he comes at us.'
'Maybe we should go after him now then?' Blowers says with a hard look, 'take the fight to him for a change.' Cookey nods seriously, Lani glances at them both before looking back to me.
'I agree,' Nick adds placing a mug down in front of Dave.
'We've got a guide now,' Clarence nods at Lani.
'Options,' I lean forward, 'we're here to get our group and get back to our fort, Darren poses a risk and will kill them and us at the first chance he gets. He could be trying to get more zombies to come after us which means we either take him out now but by doing that we put ourselves at risk or we keep going and hope we can find them before he does.'
'By which time he could have turned loads of them and be an even bigger risk, and we don't have the firepower or the resources to fight back like we did last time,' Dave replies flatly.
'And we'll be lucky to find them and get back to the boats before nightfall, and even then we've got to

hope the tide isn't out. Last night was hard enough, these shotguns are good but they take too long to re-load,' I take another drag of the cigarette.
'If we knew they'd stay slow we'd stand a good chance of getting them now,' Blowers says, 'but we know they can turn like that,' he clicks his fingers for effect.
'Pity there's not an army base we can raid again,' I mutter.
'There is,' Lani says quickly, 'there's a Territorial Army camp but it's on the other side of the Island.'
'How far is that?' Dave asks.
'Driving? Maybe an hour there and an hour back.'
'Do you know where it is?' I look at her closely.
'I know the area it's in, I went there once with my school years ago.'
'Did they have weapons?' Dave questions her, 'what did you see?'
'They had army guns,' she stares off clearly trying to think, 'like you see the soldiers with on TV.'
'Were they live firing?' Dave asks.
'What's that?' She replies.
'Could they shoot bullets?' Clarence takes over, 'did you see them being fired? Were there any targets up like on a range or anything like that?'
'Oh yeah we watched the soldiers shooting targets, they were lying down and firing down this long field with a big hill at the end, we had to wear things on our ears because of the noise.'

'Lani, when the guns were fired, did you see the bullet cases being ejected from the side of the weapon?' Clarence asks with serious intent but keeping his tone steady.

'Yeah loads of them, like in the movies,' she nods.

'Right, what are the chances that someone hasn't got there before us?' I ask, 'if they take school groups there then everyone on this Island will know, plus all the soldiers stationed here.'

'Shit, good point,' Clarence looks over at me, 'if I was local it would the first place I would head for.'

'We don't have the time to risk getting over there and finding it either looted or more likely defended and they might not take kindly to a bunch of armed men knocking on their gates. We stick to the plan, find our people and get out of here.' Nods all round although I get what they're saying and going after Darren is a tempting idea.

We fill our bags with water and whatever snack food we can fit in before shrugging the packs on and setting off again. The thought that Darren must be massing again drives us on and our pace increases until we're all sweating heavily in the blistering heat, apart from Dave and Lani who both remain looking cool and collected.

Following the shore line we walk round the long sweeping bay on the picturesque path separating the sand from the wooded area. Birds sing happily, insects and bee's buzz about merrily doing whatever insects and bee's do. They know nothing of this infection that's wiped out one species already but then I remember the rats that attacked us at the motorway service station. They were clearly infected so why not all species, why just us and rats? Surely an infection or disease can't just choose who it infects. But then there is a strong relationship between humans and rats. Rats will eat anything so if they chomped on the rotten corpses and got infected what's to stop something else eating the rats.

'What eats rats?' I ask out loud.

'Cats,' Lani answers quickly.

'Birds, foxes…dogs…anything that's hungry enough,' Clarence replies.

'The rats at the service station?' Dave asks guessing my thought process.

'Yeah, just wondering what else could get infected.'

'Everything I guess,' Nick cuts in.

'We might get zombie spiders,' Cookey shudders as Blowers bursts out laughing.

'You fucking twat! Zombie spiders!' He sputters.

'Why not?' Cookey retorts, 'they could get infected if they ate something that was infected.'

'What do spiders eat then?' Blowers goads him.

'Flies…and flies will lay eggs on anything, especially warm rotting corpses,' Cookey says.

'Well, when you put it like that,' Blowers stops laughing and stares round suspiciously at the ground as though expecting a horde of zombie spiders to suddenly launch themselves at us.

'So do you think this is manmade or what?' Cookey asks.

'What the disease or whatever it is?' Nick says, 'is it a disease or virus or infection or what?'

'I don't know mate,' I shrug, 'isn't it that a virus causes an infection? Like the virus goes from person to person and they become infected as a result.'

'So it's both?' Lani asks.

'Maybe, isn't a disease something that develops and doesn't need a virus?' Cookey replies, 'Blowers, what did your doctor say at the STD clinic?'

'He said I caught syphilis from your mum,' Blowers quips followed instantly by hoots of laughter from Nick and Lani, even Clarence chuckles deeply.

'Leave my mum out of this,' Cookey says in good humour.

'That's what the navy said that day,' Blowers quips again.

'You'd know what the navy said,' Cookey retorts, 'I bet you spent a lot of time with sailors.'

'Oh good comeback mate,' Blowers nods with respect.

'I thank you,' Cookey smiles taking a small bow.

'I think it probably is manmade,' I cut in, 'probably some bloody scientists pissing about with things they should have left alone.'

'What like terrorists?' Nick asks.

'I don't know mate,' I sigh, 'to be honest I wasn't sure where I stood on the whole terrorism thing?'

'What do you mean?' Clarence asks.

'Well I'm sure we faced a threat from people who didn't like us, meaning the west, but I just think governments can get away with murder by playing the terrorist card. Don't get me wrong, there's plenty of bloody crazy people in the world who want to kill anyone that doesn't believe in the same things as them so I guess we had to take some action, but I don't know…it just felt it was more about oil than anything else.' I realise I've just voiced an extreme view to two people who have probably devoted their lives to fighting and killing in the name of our country. Dave stays quiet and blank faced as ever but Clarence looks thoughtful.

'What about an antidote or cure, there has to be something that can fix it,' Cookey continues his questions with a keen interested look.

'It works so quickly though mate, we've all seen how fast it can take over the body, how it can evolve and change. If it was just how it started out it would be easy in theory to go out and kill them in the day and hide at night, but it changed and became different. It evolved to survive and that's just here with this threat. Imagine how else it could have changed in other places to survive other threats. We don't know how long Darren was infected before he finally turned, or why he was chosen, but we know he can speak, think and do all the things we can do…'

'So an antidote might work on one strain but not work on another, is that what you're saying?' Lani asks.
'I don't know,' I shrug feeling helpless and unable to voice the nagging fear within my mind that there will not be a cure for this. There won't be any men in white lab coats pissing about with test tubes and monkeys. This is what the world is now; two species fighting to survive. 'Keep it simple and one step at a time. We find the others and get back to the fort then worry about everything else later.'
'Amen,' Clarence rumbles.
'How much further?' I ask Lani.
'Not far, round the next bend and just a bit further on,' even she's starting to sweat now with the high heat and the sun glaring off the hot sand. The humidity feels high too and far hotter than any English summer I can remember. Rather than slowing down to take our packs off we dip into each other's bags and take bottles of water out, rehydrating from the constant sweating and anticipation of not knowing if something will happen round the next corner. Dave turns as we march along and walks backwards, lifting his hand to shield his eyes and scan the route behind us.
'Anything?'
'No Mr Howie, nothing,' He scans for a few more seconds then about turns to carry on.
'Up there,' Lani points off to a high wall butting up against the sea and what looks like a path snaking

behind it into the tree line, 'the path either goes down onto the beach or round through the grounds of the park.'

'Park?' Dave asks with concern.

'That's what it is now,' she replies, 'a park with mini golf, tennis courts and a café.'

'You said it was a fort,' Dave states with his usual diplomacy.

'It was a fort or something, maybe a battery? I heard it being called that too.'

'A mortar battery,' Dave replies.

'Yeah that.'

'Well we'll see in a minute,' reaching the end of the path we're on I can see a steep flight of stairs going down onto the beach and the high wall ahead of us. It looks solid and built in the same thick stone I saw in fort Spitbank.

'That's got to be five or six metres high,' I say as we draw closer, 'should slow them down a little.' To the right I see a path following the high wall as it disappears into the tree line. We stop to look behind us for a few minutes, each of us shielding our eyes and scanning every inch of the vista before us. The path has risen gradually as we've come along so we can see right along the sweeping bay back further than the café we stopped at. Nothing moves in my field of vision and none of the others pass remark at anything.

With a final look round we head into the darkened copse following the high wall and instantly feeling the slightly cooler shaded air. The path ends at a right angle going off to the left and we see the high wall running into a steep grass bank. Turning the corner the dirt path gives way to concrete with the high bank running along on our left and a dilapidated fence on the other side. The bank creates a funnel which would be a perfect spot to erect a barricade and prevent entry but my heart starts to sink at the lack of any signs of fortification in this place.

In silence we move forward, hands gripping our weapons and looking all around as we come out of the funnel, the high bank ends suddenly and the area in front of us opens out into a wide, modern car park. We step out into the light and see no signs of life, no fortifications, no barricades or armed sentries waiting to challenge us. On the left there are high concrete walls with multiple thick rusted metal doors embedded in them at ground level. The undulation of the walls and the mounds clearly indicate a bunker complex from the Second World War long left to fall into ruin. At the top of the concrete wall we see metal fencing and wooden benches set at intervals. Metal staircases fixed to the walls lead to the top and we see more doors and barred gates as we slowly make our way into the park.

The ground on the right opens out into a large flat grassy area with signs to enquire at the café for pitch and putt golf. A small brick built kiosk stands at the edge of a children's play area, now looking ominous and somewhat sinister in the silence of the gorgeous summer day with slides, monkey bars and swings all static and unused for several days. The construct and layout is eerily similar to that of fort Spitbank. The same conventional doorways with the same grey coloured concrete. This must have originally been a Palmerston Fort too and then adapted over the years for use in the World Wars. With the bunker rooms, high walls and funnel entrance I'm amazed that it hasn't been taken over and fortified.

'Spread out in a line, look for any signs they passed through here,' I give the instruction quietly and feel a creeping sense of unease. I expected to find our group here and I can't understand why this hasn't been put to use. The group spread out into a thin line with each person walking slowly, checking the ground, looking left and right and turning to scan behind them as they go along.

Reaching the kiosk I see another smaller car park built into the left side where the building line drops back. Up ahead is a long low single story building with big plate glass windows and the word café painted in thick black letters on the roof tiles. There are small brick built buildings standing isolated in the grounds, they look solid and well-built but have clearly been bordered up for long years with high weeds growing round the outside.

Immediately behind the kiosk is the hard surface tennis courts still with the netting in place across the middle. High metal fencing runs round the perimeter obviously to stop meandering tourists from getting whacked in the face by flying tennis balls.

'Fuck me,' Blowers mutters at the sight of the bodies stacked up in the middle of the courts and the many undead standing around them all slack jawed and drooling. At the sight of us they turn slowly and start shuffling over to the fence. I stare in horror expecting to see members of our group, or even worse my sister Sarah. We all stare over at them and I edge closer to examine each one closely. Breathing a sigh of relief I turn and shake my head at the rest, 'none of ours that I can see.' They nod back and walk over to the fence, staring in amazement at the sight of the dead and undead bodies.

'Someone's put them in there,' Dave whispers.

'Why though?' I ask. The bodies in the middle look like dead zombies judging by the injuries and emaciated withered appearance. Quite a few of them are stacked up, not neatly like Dave did in the supermarket but just heaped together. At least twenty undead are still up on their feet though groaning as they drool and bang their faces against the metal fence.

'Someone just moved in the café,' Lani whispers urgently. We spin round to face the building but see nothing other than what looks like an empty place, 'someone came to the door, saw us and darted back in,' she adds in the same hushed but rapid tone.

'Let's go and see,' I whisper back and we set off walking down the side of the chain link fence of the tennis court. The building line comes out further from the left here with a clear addition of rooms accessed by deeply recessed doors. This forms a narrow road only wide enough for one vehicle, the road runs down to the café and is bordered on the right by a chest high wooden fence which ends to show a wide grassed area in front of the café and I guess this is normally where tables and chairs would be put for the summer visitors.

'See anything?' I ask, none of them reply but keep focussed on the café with Dave and Clarence making constant sweeps all around us. We stop at the end of the fence and look over the grass to the café.

'The other entrance,' Dave nods off to the right and I see high ornate metal gates embedded into the high concrete wall. The gates are hinged to allow vehicles to enter the park area but are now closed with a thick looking chain wrapped round the middle struts.

'What's behind the café Lani,' Dave asks quietly.
'Nothing, just a back lawn and the high wall,' she answers. We move slowly across the lawn watching the front of the café and staring through

the plate glass windows at the tables and chairs inside.

'The café door's open slightly,' Dave says in muted tones as we get halfway across the lawn.

'STAND STILL AND PUT THE WEAPONS DOWN,' a loud voice booms out behind us, we spin round with Dave and Clarence instantly releasing their axes and having the skill and experience to drop and roll off, drawing pistols from their belts. Blowers and Cookey throw their axes to one side and reach back to pull their shotguns, both of them going into a crouch and stepping quickly to present a moving target. Nick jumps in front of Lani and starts moving away while also drawing his shotgun. A figure clad in black paramilitary clothing strides out of one of the deep recessed doors holding a rifle, another comes out quickly behind him.

'DAVE NO,' I bellow, as fast and loud as I can, knowing Dave could drop them both instantly. The two figures stride into the road and move their rifles between us all, aiming down from balaclava covered faces. Clad in dark overalls tucked into boots they look like something out of a Special Forces movie. Within a split second the two are covered by Dave and Clarence pointing pistols at them and the rest of us holding shotguns. They react as though surprised and seem suddenly unsure what to do.

'DROP THE GUNS,' the lead black clad figure bawls out.
'DROP YOURS OR I WILL KILL YOU BOTH,' Dave's amazing voice booms out and they both turn to stare at him.
'UP TOP,' Blowers shouts, he holds his shotgun in one hand and draws his pistol with the other, aiming one at the figures in the road and the handgun at a third black clad figure leaning over the railing and pointing another rifle down at us.
'STAND DOWN,' Dave booms out again and I watch as both the figures in the road twitch their rifles between the several targets in front of them.
'EASY, DAVE TAKE IT EASY LADS NO ONE FIRES,' I call out and both figures turn to watch me.
'Got it Mr Howie,' Dave acknowledges but keeps his pistol in a two handed grip moving swiftly between the two figures in front of him.
'Lads, nobody shoots, got it?'
'Got it,' Blowers answers but like Dave he keeps the shotgun levelled at the people in the road and the pistol pointing up at the figure above.
'We're not here for trouble,' I say to the two figures as they stare silently back at me, looking closer I can see the uniforms are unmarked and the one that hasn't spoken is trembling. 'We're looking for members of our group that might have come through here, we don't want trouble and we don't want a fight, please just lower your weapons and we'll do the same.'

'What's your name?' The lead man asks in a gruff voice.
'My name is Howie,' I take a slight step forward and lower my shotgun down to my side. The two figures glance at one another and visibly relax , gradually they lower their rifles too.
'So which one of you is Dave?' The man pulls his balaclava off to reveal a balding head and a big grin, 'they said you'd be coming.'

Chapter Four

'Fucking look at all my lovely babies,' I laugh out loud and slap Marcy hard on the backside, she looks up from her kneeling position smiling at me with fresh blood pouring down her chin, the hapless victim squirms on the ground under her iron grip and starts screaming again. I'm amazed the woman is still alive after the amount of flesh that's been ripped from her stupid fat body. We're upstairs in another house in another street. All of these houses look the same to me, fucking beige walls with beige carpets and fucking beige sofa's. Still, the colour beige really shows the blood well and I don't think we've found a house of survivors yet and not left at least one room a bloodbath.
In fact we've got so many now that they can't all fit into the houses and are stacked up outside and grumbling at not being let in to feast. I pull the curtain back and open the window to look down into the street at the hundreds of faces all turned up to stare at me. I can't see through their eyes but I can feel their devotion and loyalty to me. Like a super organism now, one part made of many and me in the middle leading them all. And this lot are different, they're fresh and strong and very hungry.
'Our babies darling,' Marcy sinks back down to finish the screaming bitch off, finally she sits back on her haunches and motions for me to take my bite. I crouch down and suck at the blood pumping

out of her fat throat. No matter how much of this I've had I still feel hungry for it. The more I had the more I wanted until it became frenzied and we ran from house to house tearing throats open and killing the little cunts as they screamed and begged. A few fuckers fought back and one even managed to kill a couple of my babies before I stepped in and threw him out of a closed window and let the rest outside tear him limb from limb.

Howie can suck my zombie balls now, he can fuck off and go blow Dave in a dark corner because while they're all reading the bible and playing goody goodies I'm here putting the hard work in and trying to make sure these poor souls have got everything they need. Just imagine if I wasn't here to look after them, what would they do? They'd suffer and maybe get a few feeds in but otherwise they'd languish outside in the heat and get all withered and dried out like prunes.

Looking up at me Marcy wipes the blood from her chin and casually looks down to examine the crimson soaked material of her blouse, frowning she pulls it away from her body but the sodden material clings to her frame. Glancing up again she takes in the state of my own filth encrusted clothes and shakes her head,

'We need clean clothes,' she sighs languidly.

'Why?'

'The leaders of the zombie army should look the part, smartness maketh the zombie,' she adds with a smile.

'I don't want clean clothes,' I examine the front of my own disgustingly putrid attire, 'we look good,' I nod smiling at her.

'No Darren, we look filthy, we're getting cleaned up and after that we're going to find some clean clothes and then have a look and see if we've got enough bodies to go after your friend Howie.'

'He's not my friend,' Instant anger flushes through me, 'he's a fucking cunt and I'm going to get my lovelies to pin him down while I take a big zombie shit in his mouth.'

'But we are going to get cleaned up first,' she says firmly, 'are you connected to me?' she asks quickly with a serious expression.

'No,' I shake my head, 'I keep trying but I can't find you and I don't know why.'

'Oh well darling, I'm sure it'll come,' she pats my arm and starts walking out of the room as the fresh corpse at my feet starts twitching. 'Well come on then,' Marcy motions with her head to follow her down the hallway to the small bathroom. Once inside she reaches into the shower cubicle and turns the spray of water on.

'Fuck off if you think I'm getting in there,' I recoil backwards towards the door, 'zombies don't wash Marcy.'

'Darren we are filthy and you smell disgusting,' she looks at me pointedly.

'No fucking way,' I shake my head, 'not happening, I like this smell,' to prove the point I pull my soaking top away from body and inhale the odour of death and metallic blood deeply and smile at her.

'Strip,' she orders.

'No chance,' folding my arms I make my stand, firm and resolute. If she thinks I'm getting under that clean fresh water she can think again.

'Fine, then you can stand there and watch,' she rips her blouse open sending the little plastic buttons pinging onto the floor. She discards the top and shrugs her tight black skirt down to stand there in black bra and panties, 'if you don't want to join me that's fine, maybe I'll go and get big boy up here to wash my back for me.' She turns away from me and reaches round to unclasp her bra, shrugging it off and letting it fall to the floor. She bends forward and pulls the panties down and my eyes fall to the smooth curve of her arse and the crusty scab forming over the bite I gave her. My undead zombie hearts starts beating faster at the sight of her naked body all covered in patches of dried blood and filth. She steps over the bath into the powerful spray of water and lets out a loud scream.

'Oh that's so cold it hurts,' she wails turning slowly round, 'it hurts so much it's so nice,' she purrs. She stops turning to stand facing me with her arms down at her side, letting me take in her naked body, the mounds of her breasts and the dark nipples, her flat stomach and the gentle curve of her hips.

'Fuck this,' I rip my own clothes off and jump into the water with her, she squeals with laughter as I yell out with the exquisite agony of freezing water pummelling my skin.

Twenty minutes later we're out of the shower using old towels to dry off and avoiding eye contact.

'Don't worry darling it's been a busy day, it happens to everyone,' she says kindly but I feel oddly flat. The extreme actions of the killing rampage, the utter depravity of going from house to house and the overwhelming urge to bite and kill left the act of sex feeling mundane and boring, I had a go but after a few minutes it went soft and to be honest I think we both felt glad it was over. Like it was some ritual we had to go through to cement our joining of minds or the traditional beginnings of a formulaic relationship. Meet a pretty girl, go out on a date and then have sex. Times are different and we are different. The urges coursing through us are not the same anymore.

'Fuck it, no offence but I'm not that bothered.'

'What?' She flares up angrily.

'Oh you're lovely and all that but that stuff we did on the street was better than trying to have proper sex.'

'I'm still a woman Darren,' she shouts.

'Not really love,' I shrug, 'you're a dead woman, a zombie, the undead, infected and diseased along with the rest of us,' she looks appalled like I just said she was fat or something, 'it is what it is.' I walk out stark naked and stroll down the stairs and out into the bright sunlight. My babies don't show any reaction to my nakedness and I feel their devotion pour from their simple dead minds. Bare feet will cause me injury so I make one of the zombies tug their shoes off and hand them over. Smart black business shoes with fine laces and they fit perfectly.
'What the fuck?' Marcy comes out behind me wearing a towel round her body, 'you can't walk round like that you look ridiculous.'
'What? Who fucking cares Marcy, this is new times and I can wear what I fucking well want.'
'Darren, you are naked wearing office shoes,' hands on hips she looks at me seriously.
'They don't care,' I nod to the mass of undead drooling away nearby, 'and anyone with enough mind left to notice what I'm wearing will be dead within a few minutes anyway so fuck 'em.'
'I'm not going anywhere with you dressed like that.'
'Well I'm not putting anything else on, take that towel off and let the air get to your body, it feels wonderful and liberating.'
'No way!'
'Why not?'

'Because they'll see,' she nods at the horde and clutches the towel tighter round her bosoms.
'Marcy they don't care, they're just like dogs now. They couldn't give a fuck if we dressed as clowns.' She looks suspiciously at the horde watching to see if they stare at her, slowly she plucks the corner of the towel out and lets the garment fall to the ground.
'See, are any of them perving over you?' I stare round at the horde who have shown no reaction whatsoever to Marcy standing there in the buff.
'Big boy is staring,' Marcy looks at the hulking teenage zombie staring at her with utter awe.
'He always stares at you anyway, he's got a thing for motherly types so let him have a thrill.'
'Motherly types? I'm not that fucking old!'
'No I mean you turned him and stroked his face when he went under and came back so he probably sees you like a mother figure, like he did with his step-mum.'
'He was having sex with his step-mum,' she replies coldly.
'Well yeah… fuck it, I know what I mean.'
'I think he's getting an erection Darren,' Marcy watches the bulge grow in the groin of the roided zombie man child.
'So he is, dirty fucker.'
'At least he finds me attractive,' she mutters.
'I find you attractive, very attractive.'

'He shows it,' she points at the now stiffened tent peg straining against his stained jogging bottoms.
'Well go and fuck him then,' I say exasperated.
'Maybe I will,' she retorts quickly.
'Do that and I'll cut his dick off and stuff it down his throat.'
'Oh so you can get jealous then?'
'I'm the super zombie so he can look all he wants but he doesn't get to touch what's mine.'
'Yours?' She asks archly.
'Mine Marcy,' I stare at her defiant eyes.
'Ours,' she hisses at me.
'Mine,' I growl back.
'Ours Darren, you'd be fucking dead by now if it wasn't for me, you'd have charged after them and blundered about getting killed and ruining everything. It was my idea to turn this lot, my idea,' her voice screams out making the veins in her neck bulge out.
'I meant you're mine not them,' I wave my arm at the horde all standing there patiently, 'they're ours but you're mine.'
'Oh I thought you meant they're yours,' she calms instantly.
'No you're mine they're ours.'
'You just said that.'
'I'm saying it again.'
'Well I'm glad we got that cleared up now can we please get on, we've still got a lot left to do.'
'Like what,' I ask confused as hell.

'We need more bodies,' she says as though talking to a simpleton.

'We've got loads,' turning round I make a point of looking at the horde crammed into the front garden and backed up in the street all across the road. Most of them have been turned by me or Marcy but others are zombies that were already here and have tagged along for the ride.

'We should get more,' she says stiffly crossing her arms.

'Oh Marcy can't we just go and get Howie now?'

'No Darren, we're doing it properly this time. There will be time for playing later but we're going to keep going until it I think we have enough.'

'Oh fucking hell! That'll take ages...'

'Stop your whining and get on with it,' still naked she strides past me through the gate and into the road, 'and put some bloody trousers on.'

CHAPTER FIVE

'We thought it was you but we had to be sure,' the balding man says, the second man has pulled his balaclava off to reveal a hard face topped with thick brown hair. We're standing round with weapons held down at our sides, still not confident enough to put them away just yet and I can sense Dave and Clarence keeping a discrete distance.
'Howie, good to meet you,' I extend my hand out to the balding man who swaps the gun over to free his right hand up.
'Dean, that's my café behind you, your group are with us safe and sound,' he shakes hands firmly and steps back to look round at us, finally settling his gaze on Lani, 'you're a local aren't you,' he asks with a puzzled expression.
'She is, we met her down the road,' I reply quickly, 'where are our group? Can we see them?'
'They're downstairs in the bunkers, we'll take you down…has anyone followed you?'
'No,' Dave says firmly staring hard at Dean.
'Let's get under cover quickly, follow me,' Dean turns to head back towards the recessed door he appeared from.
'Before we go, what are they doing there?' I point towards the tennis courts.
'I'll tell you once we're inside, not here,' Dean replies moving back towards the door.

'I'd rather know now mate,' the others take their lead from me and remain still.

'It's not safe out here, we should get undercover,' Dean says quickly.

'No offence mate but we don't know you or what's in there,' I feel the tension rising again and although Dave hasn't moved an inch I can tell he's poised to react.

'I understand, Mike go and get someone from his group and bring them up,' Dean turns back to me then glances at the tennis courts, 'we're trying to see how long they survive without food or water.'

'And?' I ask.

'Some of them have been in there since the first night it happened,' he replies.

'What about the dead ones? What happened to them?'

'Some died on their own and we chucked in another few bodies to see if they would eat their own or what would happen. But they haven't touched the corpses. We put cups of water in there and they ignored them, then we chucked fresh and rotten animal meat in but they ignored that too.'

'Do they change at night?' Clarence asks.

'They howl like the rest of them, and then get faster and meaner chucking themselves at the fence. We put a guard out to make sure they don't break the fence down.'

'Howie!' Sarah comes running out of the door straight into my arms. The shock hits me hard and I hug her fiercely feeling tears stinging my eyes. 'Sarah, oh thank god,' I hear the others crowding in, she breaks free and hugs them each in turn and even Dave doesn't object to the physical contact. Finally she grabs Clarence and throws her arms round his huge chest. He blushes bright red but returns the embrace lifting her clean off her feet in a giant bear hug.

'Oh Howie,' she says again when Clarence finally releases her, 'we thought you'd be gone, we thought all of you would be gone,' tears spill from her eyes as we hug again. 'What happened at the end? Where's Tucker and the others?' She looks round and see's the desperately sad looks of the lads.

'They didn't make it,' I shake my head and feel tears falling down my own cheeks, looking over I see Blowers and Cookey have also gone red eyed and silent.

'Howie! Dave! Thank god for that,' Ted comes striding out of the door and clasps my hand with both of his.

'Ted, oh it's good to see you mate,' I smile with genuine pleasure and shake his hand vigorously, 'come here you bloody hero,' Ted gives me a brief hug before breaking free to greet each of us in turn, shaking hands and seeing the tears falling from all of us. Lani stares bemused at the emotive re-union.

Within seconds more of our group are pouring from the door, Sergeant Hopewell, Tom and Steven, Terri and more faces we last saw in the fort when they were running for their lives out of the rear gate.
I catch a quick glimpse of Dean standing there shrugging at his mate, both of them look worried and I know we should do as they ask but seeing our group takes over anything else.
Blowers, Cookey and Nick get treated like the hero's they are, and I watch them crying with bitter sweet sorrow, relief, happiness heart wrenching sadness as we're all bombarded with people asking who survived, women and children demanding to know if their husbands, fathers or brothers lived or died. To this group we are the returning heroes who survived something that none of us expected to walk away from. The horror and desperation we faced on that battle field we faced for them, so they would live and have a chance of freedom. They know this and the strain they must have been under since they left is huge, and to see us now brings those emotions out in all of us.
Sobbing and crying I try desperately to answer people as they ask about their loved ones but I simply didn't know the names of all of the men we fought alongside. There wasn't time to learn them. In the end Sergeant Hopewell and Ted assert their natural authority and start herding them back inside the door. As the crowd grows thinner a few

of us are left standing close together, tears drying and I see Sarah hugging a crying Clarence as he tells her about the loss of Malcolm. Blowers, Cookey and Nick are all being patted and hugged as they talk of Tucker, Curtis and Jamie laying down their lives while Steven, Tom, Terri and Jane all listen intently.

'You made it then,' Ted says with fatherly pride to me.

'Just about, it was awful Ted,' I shake my head at the memory, 'we lost so many, so many, I don't know how to tell them,' I motion towards the backs of the women and children filing back into the doorway.

'They're expecting it,' Ted says bluntly, 'we didn't expect to see any of you again.'

'Er, I'm sorry but I really would prefer it if we got back inside,' Dean comes forward speaking politely.

'Of course mate, I'm so sorry.'

'No we understand we've heard all about you and what happened over there but we've kept this place pretty clear up till now and we'd rather keep it that way.'

'Come through Howie, you'll be amazed at this place,' Ted starts ushering the others inside and I wait at the back to go through with Dave.

'That was intense,' I mutter quietly to him.

'Good to see them all again though Mr Howie,' Dave gives a rare smile, 'your sister looks well.'

'They've obviously been well looked after.'
'Come through,' Dean stands a few feet into the recessed area holding a thick barred gate open and motioning us to enter. We do as we're told and enter a long tunnel. Dean pulls the gate closed and fastens thick bolts home on the inside then big padlocks at the top and bottom. Finally he steps in and then closes a thick wooden door sealing in darkness, a torch lights up within a few seconds and we watch him ramming more bolts home before squeezing past us and leading the way through the dark tunnel.
'The battery was built back in the 1850's but then during the world war's they added more tunnels and bunkers. They used it for all sorts of secret testing back in the day, before the council closed most of them up and said they'd all fallen in or collapsed. We broke through when this happened and found nearly all of them were perfectly fine. There's a whole network of tunnels connecting rooms and bunkers. We've managed to get loads of food and bottled water down here.'
'Thank you for taking our group in Dean,' the air is musty but it feels much cooler down here and I realise the winding tunnel is going downhill and getting a bit steeper every few metres.
'We didn't have much choice if I'm honest, they turned up making a whole load of noise and that Sergeant woman and your sister promised they would only stay for a few days...we couldn't just

leave them out there to die,' Dean shrugs as he walks ahead of us. The dark tunnel turns to the right and opens into a large room illuminated by the glow of many candles and lanterns. The room is sectioned off with distinct bundles of bedding and clothing marking out separate sleeping areas. A cacophony of voices reaches us from the many women either sitting or standing around talking. Some children run about in excitement and others sit in forlorn shock looking pale and drawn. Faces turn to stare as we file through following Dean and the others ahead of him. Doors lead off to more rooms crammed with people sitting, lying or standing about quietly talking.

We follow Dean through more tunnels, these ones lit by hanging gas lanterns or strings of fairy lights strung up and connected to car batteries. We enter another large room again filled with women and children, and pass more, smaller rooms these ones clearly filled with local people who have had time to gather belongings from home or other places, bedding and soft furnishings, pictures of loved ones, shelves of books and children's toys. There are more men here and it's clear the best rooms have been reserved for the locals who got here first.

Dean shows us to a large central room stocked with tinned food and bottled water. A guard armed with a shotgun sits on a chair reading an old newspaper,

he nods amiably as we pass into yet more rooms filled with food, water, cans of beer and spirits. 'We've been out foraging and bringing supplies in every day. We've avoided this town and gone into the villages to raid houses, pubs, shops and anything else we can find. There's a fresh water supply in here too, drawn from somewhere deep underground. We use that mainly and keep the bottles in case it runs dry or something. We've got a few nurses and a vet but no doctor yet, but we did manage to get into a couple of pharmacies and doctors surgeries and empty the shelves so we've got medicines, anti-biotics and penicillin.
Bandages are boiled and sterilised then re-sealed and we allow body washes every few days on a rotation basis.'
'How many have you got down here?' I ask amazed at the effort that's already gone into setting all this up.
'We had a couple of hundred before your lot arrived so now we're bursting,' he stops and looks back at me seriously, 'will you be able to take them away today or tomorrow?'
'Definitely mate, as soon as we can get them back to the boats and the tide is right.'
'We don't mind having them and we've got enough food and water but, well you know how it is,' his voice trails off diplomatically.
'I can imagine Dean, you've got a good set up here and why should you take in strangers.'

'Sounds harsh and I apologise for that but survival is just that...survival.' Through more tunnels and we reach another large room, this one clearly used by Dean and his family or closest friends. A large table and chairs in the middle and more doors running round the edge of the room, most of them closed but the few open reveal beds, easy chairs, and stacks of food and water. Sergeant Hopewell and the others are all standing in the main middle room waiting as Dave and I file in. One side of the table is reserved for Dave, Clarence me and the lads. We all sit down as trays of hot coffee are brought out from one of the rooms and placed on the table. Dean and a few members of his black clad group take seats opposite us, everyone else either grabs a free chair or leans against the walls. More people emerge until the room is nearly full with everyone waiting for our account. I see Lani watching us and I give her a smile and a nod, she must know some of the people down here already but I can see she's positioned herself so she's close to the lads sitting at the end of the table.

A silence descends after we've grabbed coffee mugs and taken a few sips, added sugar and stirred them round. The room feels hot and muggy with so many people crammed together and breathing in the confined area. Expectant faces stare at me, people want the full story and not just the snatched bits they got outside.

Taking a deep breath I start to relay the account from when they left the fort, the battle, the fighting and who I knew we lost, who survived, all the rows of injured people stacked up inside the fort when we came back through. I tell them how Darren escaped and how we figured they'd come here then how we saw Darren last night and the fight in the hotel. Clarence jumps in a few times when he senses me going quiet and trying to get my thoughts in order, Blowers too adds bits here and there. We explain the whole thing until we met Lani and started working our way along to here. At the mention of Lani's name everyone turns to stare at her, she goes poker faced and nods once in greeting before staring out with the same expressionless face I've seen on Dave so many times.

'So you think they're massing now?' Dean asks leaning forward.

'Yes,' Dave answers in his flat voice, 'he will be turning as many as he can before it gets to night then he'll come for us.'

'How will he know where you are?' Dean asks.

'He must have access to local knowledge by now,' Dave answers, he leans forward to stare at Dean, 'I think from the way he controlled all of his people before, he must be able to get in their heads or something, and if he finds those things you've got in the tennis courts he'll know you're here.'

'He can try all he wants, this place is locked up tight,' Dean answers confidently, more of his group nod in agreement.
'What about you?' I ask, 'how come you're dressed like that?'
'Believe it or not,' he smiles, 'I ran a zombie event in the park every year, Park of The Dead we called it, we got loads of people dressed up and took customers round on a sort of themed walk. We had uniformed soldiers as part of the show,' he shrugs with a sheepish smile, 'we figured we might as well put them to use.'
'Bloody hell mate, talk about reality and fantasy merging.'
'Yeah something like that,' he laughs in good humour.
'What weapons do you have?' Dave asks and I almost chuckle at the scripted way he thinks. Fortification, defence, weapons, food fluid and rest.
'Shotguns rifles and loads of ammunition, that's it.'
'Er…if this Darren is gathering loads of them zombie things to come here for them,' one of the women cuts in from behind Dean, 'why are we letting them stay here? I don't mean to be rude but they're putting everyone else at risk.'
'That's a good point,' Dean turns to me, 'if you go now we might be able to survive without being found.'
'True…'

'Won't happen,' Dave cuts in, 'Darren is here now, even if we wait outside so he can eat us alive, he won't stop at that.'

'But if it's you he wants,' the woman asks in a blunt tone.

'It is,' Dave replies, 'until he gets us then what? What do you think he will do then?'

'But you being here is putting us at risk,' the woman's voice rises and several of her group nod in agreement.

'It's late afternoon now, the tide was in this morning so I'm guessing it's out now. We have to wait until it comes back in before we can get the boats out. There's nothing we can do until then,' I try to explain politely, I can see her point and if I was in her place I would be thinking exactly the same.

'It'll be getting dark by the time the tide comes back in, and by that time he'll have every fucking zombie here trying to get in, Dean do something,' she shouts.

'What? I can't just kick them out, you heard what he said…the tides out so they can't use the boats and we can't leave them outside until night.'

'And what about when they get here?' Another voice shouts from the back, 'what then?' More voices join in with both sides arguing amongst themselves.

'QUIET,' Dean bangs on the table a few times until the shouting dies down, 'I'm sorry Howie but they're right, if you stay here and we get surrounded then we can't get in or out until they either go away or die...and judging by the ones in the tennis court they'll last a long time. It puts us all at risk.' Silence descends again and the tension rises, it seems clear to me what we have to do. I look at Dave who nods in agreement then down the row at Clarence, Nick, Blowers and Cookey. They can see it too, what needs to be done and they nod back at me.

'Then we'll go and meet them,' I say to a stunned room. Leaning forward I look Dean in the eye, 'we'll go and meet them before they get here but you promise me that you'll get our people to their boats as soon as it's safe.'

'Howie no!' Sarah shouts in shock, more voices join in but we sit there resolute knowing there is no other choice. We've come this far to protect them, why fail now.

'Are you serious?' Dean asks with a puzzled look.

'Yes mate, we'll go out and head them off. If we can find somewhere defensible and get them round us then like you said there's no reason for them to come here and find you.'

'That's suicide Howie,' Ted shouts angrily.

'We can draw them inland,' Clarence's deep voice rumbles through the melee of noise, 'if we lure them away from here and keep them busy for a few hours then it gives Dean a chance to get everyone to the boats in the morning.'

'Sounds good to me mate,' I nod back, 'lads?' I look down knowing what they'll say but a twisted part of me wants this lot to see just how brave these lads are, and what the word sacrifice really means.
'I'm in Mr Howie,' Nick says with a smile.
'Don't even need to ask Mr Howie,' Cookey gives a big grin then takes a nonchalant glance round the room.
'It'll give us a chance to fuck Darren up too,' Blowers adds with a nod.
'Dave?' I stare at Dean and look along the faces of the people staring back in shock and confusion.
'Yes Mr Howie?'
'You up for another scrap mate?'
'Do you need to ask Mr Howie?'
'You're not doing that again,' Sarah shouts in blind anger, 'not again Howie, you did it once and that was enough. We stay together from now on.'
'She's right Howie, all of you,' Ted says firmly.
'Er…may I say something?' Lani suddenly speaks up, her voice strong and confident, every face turns to look at her, 'we've only seen them slow in the day but fast at night right?' She looks round getting nods from most of the room, 'but you said Mr Howie, that they can switch quickly and get faster during the day too, right?'
'That's right.'
'But you also said that they don't appear to be able to sustain that frantic pace for long, that it weakens them and makes them easier to kill, right?'

'Yeah,' I nod back at her unsure of where's she going with this.

'And you also said this place is locked up tight, right?' She looks at Dean who nods back.

'So why not let them come here and go crazy all night, really get them going and get them exhausted then when daylight comes and they get slow we go out and kill them, and like you said Mr Howie, if they're still fast then they'll be weaker.'

Another stunned silence fills the room.

'Why didn't you think of that Dave?' I ask quietly.

'Sorry Mr Howie…it's a good idea though,' rare praise from Dave but Lani doesn't know him well enough to understand the raised eyebrows from the rest of our group.

'Very good idea, but only if Dean and his group agree, if not then we honour their decision and take the fight straight to Darren.'

'Agreed,' Lani says with a nod then looks round at us all staring at her, 'sorry, I just er…'

'Dean?' He nods several times deep in thought staring past me, 'let me have five minutes to see what my…er….people think,' he hesitates on calling them his people, like he is uncomfortable with the division of entities. Them and us, not just people but tribes distinct and diverse.

'We're all people,' Sarah picks up on the mood, 'we all have a right to life and we should work together not cast each other out, we wouldn't do that to you if you came to our fort.'

'She's right,' a man with a rich baritone voice steps forward, 'I won't stand by and watch you throw these people out and if they go to fight then I'll go with them,' he turns to address the crowd gathered behind Dean, his rich voice fills the room and he speaks like a barrister or someone used to addressing the public. 'We can hide in here forever but going on what we've heard it's only a matter of time before they come for us. Our children need sunlight and air, we need to plant food and think of the future, hiding down here won't get that done. We need to accept this has happened and make decisions that benefit all of us, and when I say all of us I mean the people that are left and not just our so called group down here.'

'You're wrong,' the woman shouts, she is middle aged with a stern face, 'we took the time and effort to make this place suitable so we have the right to be safe here.'

'What if this place became unusable,' Sarah cuts in quickly, 'what would you do then? If you knew there was another safe place nearby?'

'That's not the point,' the woman shouts back.

'It's exactly the point, the man with the baritone voice interjects, 'if we lost this place then we'd have to go and ask for help from somewhere else and that could happen!'

'Why put ourselves and our children at risk for people we don't know,' the woman shouts louder clearly annoyed at having a member of her own group turn on her.

'But we do know them,' the man replies, 'they're here and we've met them so we do know them. What's next? We start having tribal fort war's at the same time as fighting the zombies out there. This is utterly ridiculous. We should be out there doing what we can to get rid of them.'

'Don't be so bloody stupid,' the woman screams with blind fury, 'are you suggesting that we go out there and hunt them down? Have you seen what they're capable off?'

'Howie,' the man turns to me suddenly, 'how many have you killed?'

'Me personally or all of us together?'

'Your group, how many?'

'Bloody hell, Dave could probably tell you the actual number…er…'

'Twelve thousand four hundred and twenty eight,' Dave says flatly.

'Jesus mate have you really been counting them?' Our whole group stares at him shocked.

'No, I made it up. I don't know how many,' Dave gives a very small smile which causes Blowers, Cookey, Nick and I to burst out laughing at the exceptionally rare attempt at humour from this quiet man

'Sorry, I don't know but it's got to be thousands. We killed loads just travelling round but then we

had that big fight a couple of days ago and that would have wiped out several thousand of them.'
'More than that,' Clarence says thoughtfully, 'if you think about what you told us about Salisbury, then London, then our commune and the last fight...' He trails off with both eyebrows raised.
'Think how many the GPMG took out,' Nick adds.
'And those trenches we blew up,' Cookey muses.
'The housing estate...that must have killed a couple of thousand on its own,' Nick rubs his chin thinking.
'Yeah, fair one,' I nod back and turn to look round at the people staring at me, 'we've probably taken out tens of thousands then.'
'With how many of you?' The man asks like a friendly barrister cross examining a star witness.
'Not that many really, we lost a few here and there but on the whole we've stayed remarkably intact for such a small group. Don't get me wrong we lost thousands during that big fight outside our fort but we killed far far more than we lost and what we've gained from that is a real chance of living safely for a while, and it's not just that but we learnt how to fight them, what hurts them, when to stand our ground and when to retreat...I guess more than anything we learnt not to fear them entirely,' I look round to see everyone hanging on my words, 'they're frightening and all that, truly terrifying really but they're not the super human monsters you think they are. You've seen what they're like in

the daytime from your tennis court experiment, bloody hell any one of my lot could take down a horde three or four times that size with just a knife if they stayed like that,' I sense the lads all sitting up higher at the compliment.

'But the real strength is having complete faith in your mates beside you,' Clarence jumps in, his deep voice and large frame mesmerising the people watching us, 'knowing that they'll stand on the line and hold their courage.'

'Bloody hell, you said you've loads of shotguns here,' I look directly at Dean who nods in response, 'they are devastating to a packed horde, form a couple of lines up and have synchronised firing, front line fires while the rear line loads and just blast them away, use the multiple exits you've got here to run out shoot a load and get back in, then find another door and do it again. Darren's only got a day so even he can't muster that many.'

'Thousand at the most,' Dave adds and I wish he hadn't because a thousand sounds like a massive number, it is a massive number and I groan inwardly as mouths start to drop open at hearing it.

'A thousand?' the woman asks loudly.

'At the most,' Dave shrugs.

'Dean. You've heard what these men have said,' the man with the rich voice picks up his thread quickly, 'even if they do bring a thousand…or five thousand it means we can finish them off and have a chance at living in safety.' I look at Dean who remains expressionless, clearly thinking hard.

'Mate, whatever you decide we'll stand by, if you want us to go out and head them off we will on the condition that you promise to get our group to the boats as soon as possible.'

'You'd go out against a thousand of them?' Dean asks me seriously.

'Yes.'

'At night?'

'Yes mate…have you seen Dave fight? Trust me the odds aren't that bad.'

'What that little thing?' the woman's scornful tones cut through the room as the lads all take a sharp intake of breath and I glance over to see Sarah, Ted and the officers all looking shocked. Only Dave stays as devoid of expression as ever.

'That *little thing* has probably killed more of them than the rest of us put together,' Clarence's voice seethes with anger, going red in the face he stands up his massive frame seeming to dominate the room. The lads stand with him and look equally as angered, 'that *little thing* is the bravest man I have ever met and I've been in more combat zones than you could count,' he leans forward and presses his fists into the table which creaks under his weight, 'and *that little thing* would willingly go out there alone against ten thousand if he was asked. Excuse me…I need some air.' He turns to find a sudden gap opening up which he strides through with Sarah hot on his heels.

'I think we all do,' I reply, 'sorry to ask but have you got sentries or look outs posted?'

'Yeah all round,' Dean replies.

'Good then we're going outside to cool off and let you talk in peace,' we turn to file out and I wait to hear someone say we can't go outside but thankfully they seem distracted and no one yells after us. As I walk through the first tunnel the man with the rich voice runs to catch up with me.

'Paul,' he extends a hand to shake, 'I'm sorry about that but tensions are high as you can see.'

'Nice to meet you Paul, don't worry but that woman was getting offensive and after what we've been through you can't blame the lads for reacting that way.'

'God no, I'm amazed you stayed as cool as you did, listen we'll have a proper chat and come and find you when it's done.'

'Thanks mate I appreciate that.'

'Dean is a very decent man, he might have looked quiet back there but the man has a steel rod running through his core.' We leave Paul in one of the big rooms to head back and speak to Dean while we thread our way through the complex of tunnels and bunkers. Word spreads as we go through that we're going outside and suddenly many people are heading for the doors and exits.

'They've been cooped up in here since this began,' Ted explains as we walk through the darkened tunnels.

'Shit I'm starting to wish I hadn't said we're going out now, it'll just look like we're trying to undermine Dean.'

'I don't think you could stop them if you tried Howie,' Ted replies with a smile. We follow the crowds out through a different route to a door further back in the park, coming out into the car park and I see our inner group all standing to one side. Some of the local guards look very unhappy at nearly all the fort's residents suddenly pouring out for a few minutes of sunshine and fresh air. Standing together we look over at children racing to the play area, screaming and yelling with delight while worried looking parents run after them telling them to be quiet.

'Hey mate,' I shout up at one bemused looking guard standing on the top of the wall, 'we'll go to the top where we came in and keep guard if you want.'

'Cheers mate,' the man smiles and gives a thumbs up before speaking into a small radio fastened to the front of his black overalls.

We file through the car park towards the entrance, looking round I see nearly our whole group here. The officers, Sarah and Clarence, the lads and Lani, Dave and even that woman that helped Sarah in the back of the van on the way from London to the fort.

Steven and Tom both keep sneaking glances at the sawn off shotguns wedged into the backpacks of the lads and looking down at their own full length double barrelled weapons.
We find a spot on the grassy area by the pitch and putt and settle down in a wide semi-circle angled to watch the entrance path.
'I'll go and have a quick look up there Mr Howie,' Dave says indicating the path.
'I'll come with you,' Lani adds quickly. Nodding at both of them I wonder why she's chosen our group to stand by when surely this lot would have taken her in seeing as she's a local.
'Howie you can't be serious at going to head them off, that was a bloody stupid thing to say,' Sarah wastes no time in voicing her opinion.
'What choice do we have?'
'Plenty of choices Howie,' Sergeant Hopewell cuts in, 'I see where you're coming from but you've already marched out to battle once and no one is expecting you to do it again.'
'I disagree,' Blowers interrupts, 'if this lot don't want us and they get all nasty then they could make life very hard for our people. If it means they get a chance of getting back safely then we have to do it.'
'Simon you don't have to keep saving everyone,' Sarah replies.
'Simon? Who's Simon?' I ask confused.
'Me, that's my first name,' Blowers laughs.

'Shit, I'd forgotten you even had one.'
'Stop changing the subject Howie,' Sarah chides as Nick and Cookey both laugh and start ragging Blowers by calling him Simon.
'Sarah, we're not being heroes but if it has to be done then so be it.'
'You lot are getting addicted to killing them thats what it is,' Sarah says firmly, 'I could see it in your faces before that big fight and downstairs, it's like a thrill to you, being all heroic and going out against thousands of them like that.'
'No it's not,' Clarence cuts across her.
'Then what is it because I don't understand. Surely it would be better to sit and wait it out here than risk dying again, how many chances do you need?' She looks round first at Clarence then me and finally at the lads, 'how many times are you going to risk your lives? Until every zombie is dead? Are you going to go out and kill all of them? Just you few?'
'Nah, we'll just send Dave,' Cookey mutters.
'Don't be funny Alex,' Sarah retorts quickly and I watch as Cookey sinks lower from the sudden tongue lashing, 'right I'll tell you what,' she looks round at us again, 'if you go out there then I'm coming with you.'
'Oh hang on…' I start to say getting cut off by protests from the others too.
'And me,' Terri speaks for the first time and I can see from her face that she means it.

'Oh no just wait a minute…'
'Me too,' Ted looks as serious as the others.
'All of us,' Sergeant Hopewell joins in.
'Can we saw our shotgun ends off too?'
'Be quiet Steven.'
'Sorry Sarge.'
'For fuck's sake,' I say exasperated.
'What?' Terri asks, 'what is it Howie? If you're saying that it's so important to save these women and children that you'd go out and fight another battle then why not us too?'
'Well because…'
'We don't have children,' she adds without letting me speak, 'we're just as capable as you at fighting and defending our group, we can shoot guns and swing axes about the same as you can.'
'None of you are combat trained,' Clarence replies quickly but gets shot down instantly by Sarah.
'He's a supermarket manager,' she points at me, 'and they were on their first day in the army,' she moves her pointing hand to the lads.
'But they've got experience now,' he rumbles.
'And how did they get that experience?' Terri asks, 'by being herded away and kept safe? No? By getting out there and fighting that's bloody how.'
'I agree,' Lani adds in her strong confident voice, 'I've only just joined and I'm sorry for interrupting,' she adds.
'Don't be sorry,' Sarah smiles up at her, 'here sit down, I'm Sarah.'

'But I've killed a few of them and I've already decided that if you go out there then I'm coming too.'
'Why?' Nick asks quickly.
'They killed my family, they killed everyone I know so why is it just your right to get revenge?' Lani replies looking up, proud and defiant.
'It's not about revenge,' I say.
'Yes it is,' Sergeant Hopewell cuts in, 'when you and Dave came to the police station that day you said you had to find your sister, but you found her Howie and now she's safe so why keep going?'
'Well because she needs to get back to the fort,' I reply weakly.
'Oh that's big of you,' Sarah growls at me, 'why do I need to get back? Why am I different to everyone else here?'
'Ah this is getting silly,' I throw my hands up.
'Dave what do you think?' Sarah turns to Dave sitting quietly next to me. He looks at me for long seconds blank faced before answering.
'Men fight. Always have done. Men fight to protect their families and what they hold dear. Men fight for all sorts of reasons but that's just the way it is…'
'Thank you Dave,' I smile feeling like I've won the point.
'…But so do women,' he adds to my audible groan, 'women fight harder than men when they need to, women can be ferocious in battle, ask Clarence.'
The big man nods reluctantly.

'Cheers Dave,' I groan.
'That's okay Mr Howie.'
'I was being sarcastic.'
'I know.'
'Well I'm glad that's cleared up then,' Sarah smiles triumphantly and I look round to see nearly everyone grinning and Ted shaking his head with a small knowing smile.
'You walked into that one son,' he says.
'Yeah I get that impression.'
'So can we saw the ends off now?' Steven asks hopefully.
'Yes mate, if we all go out together then you can saw the ends off.'
'Brill!' He sounds delighted and gets a stern look of disapproval from the Sergeant. Clarence and I exchange unhappy glances and he shrugs his huge shoulders like two boulders lifting up and down.
'If nothing else it's worth it to see that,' Ted says after a few minutes silence. I follow his gaze to the playground and the children running about freely. Some of the parents join in on the monkey bars and roundabout, others stand around with a mixture of happy and worried faces. Their laughter and giggles sound out into the quiet summer air and I can imagine this place being crammed during a normal summer day. A ball gets kicked onto the grass and bounces over towards us and I watch Nick starting to shrug his backpack off discretely. Cookey catches the movement and starts doing the

same, both of them speeding up to beat the other one until Lani ditches her bag into the middle and sprints past them laughing. With shouts they burst up and start sprinting for the ball as Blowers slowly stubs his cigarette out and starts taking his pack off too. Lani reaches the ball first and kicks it back to the children just as she's joined by Nick and Cookey. Within seconds a game has started with items of clothing being set down as goals and the children trying to beat our group. More children come running up as Steven and Tom both join in too, laughing and calling for the ball.

'Looks like they need a goalie,' Clarence surprises us all by jogging over leaving the rest of us now minding several axes, shotguns and backpacks.

'When did you start smoking again?' Sarah calls out as she catches me lighting one up and blowing a lazy plume of smoke out.

'Er...today actually.'

'It's bad for you,' she chides.

'So are zombies,' I retort quickly. Clarence takes over in goal, squatting down to get ready for some saves until one plucky child shouts that he's too big and the goal has to be made bigger.

'There's Dean,' Dave nods past me at the approaching man accompanied by several of his group. Getting slowly to my feet I walk a few paces forward and watch as he tells his friends to wait and walks on to speak with me alone. Greeting me with a nod he stands watching the children play for a couple of minutes and I get the impression he's still trying to make a final decision.

'It would have been okay if he hadn't mentioned there could be a thousand of them,' he says finally. 'I don't know where he got that number from Dean.'

'It is possible though isn't it?'

'Yeah it is,' I sigh already knowing what the answer is. We lock eyes for a second and I feel pleased that despite the bad news he has the decency to look me in the eye.

'I'm sorry Howie but we put it to a vote and well...'

'Don't worry mate, I pretty much expected it.'

'If it's any consolation I voted for you to stay but they just got hung up on the thought of a thousand of those things coming this way.'

'Yeah fair one,' if it hadn't been for Sarah and the others saying they'd be coming with us it wouldn't bother me so much, but the thought of leading my sister and the rest of them into a fight like that is just awful. Looking over I see them all staring at me and Dean and I wonder if they can work out what's being said from our body language.

'But we still honour the promise of getting the rest of them to the boats as soon as possible.'

'Okay mate, I appreciate that. Listen, there's a few more that are coming out with us now. Have you got any spare weapons we can take?'

'We can spare a few shotguns and some ammunition and we've got a couple of other bits and pieces too. I'll get them ready for you.'

'Cheers mate, no hard feelings,' I extend my hand which he takes with a firm grasp.

'So you've given him the bad news then?' Paul says as he strides towards us, a sour expression twisting his features.

'It's no problem Paul, we did make the offer in the first place.'

'I think it's fucking terrible,' he spits, 'and I stand by what I said too, I will be going with you and so will a few others.'

'Paul…' Dean turns to the man with a worried look.

'No Dean it's not on, it's just not on,' Paul waves his hand as his voice rises, 'it's utterly barbaric to send these people out and let them do the dangerous work so we can stay in safety here. You heard what they said; those fucking things will come for us no matter if these people are here or not.'

'Paul we put it to a vote,' Dean says patiently and I can tell he doesn't really believe in what he's saying.

'Yes we did Dean, but that doesn't mean I have to like it and I made it perfectly clear that if you chose to send them out then I would be going too.'

'That's your decision Paul,' Dean sighs walking off, his shoulders slumped in defeat 'I'll get some weapons ready Howie.'

'Thank you,' with a sinking heart I wait for Dean to leave then glance over to see Clarence and Dave both staring at me. My look tells them everything they need to know and they both nod back at me.
'We'd better get ready,' I say to Paul. Suddenly feeling there's nothing else to say I walk away back towards my group. Clarence, Dave and the lads walk across to intercept me.
'We're going out then?' Clarence asks wiping sweat from his face.
'Yep,' my response is curt.
'I don't want them to come with us,' he growls with quiet intensity, 'it doesn't feel right.
'I agree Mr Howie,' Nick adds quickly, 'no offence but we've got this far together and we know how to fight alongside each other.'
'Look at last night, we held fucking shit loads of them off for hours on our own,' Cookey swears with as much intensity as Clarence.
'I don't like it any more than you do,' I reply watching Sarah and the others looking at us.
'We could get them inside and just move out quickly,' Clarence urges, 'get Dean or whoever to lock the doors up and not let them out.'
'She'll go fucking nuts,' they all know I mean Sarah.
'She can go nuts but at least she'll be alive,' Clarence says.
'They're coming over,' Blowers mutters quietly. Turning round to face them we couldn't look guiltier if we tried and I watch Sarah's facial

expression change as she gets close enough to speak.

'I know exactly what you're thinking and it won't bloody work,' she looks at each of us in turn.

'Dean said we can stay the night,' Cookey tries lying but it falls instantly flat and his voice trails off as Sarah, Terri and Sergeant Hopewell fix him with a trio of hard stares.

'Did he?' Sergeant Hopewell asks Cookey quietly but the tone leaves no doubt of her ability to see through him.

'No...' Cookey mumbles looking down and we all feel the same guilt for trying to deceive them.

'Right, so we're going out to meet them, 'a statement not a question as Terri looks straight at me.

'I'm not having this,' Clarence draws himself up to his full height, plants his feet apart, folds his massive arms and inflates his chest to stare down at them.

'Not having what?' Sarah smiles at him sweetly, skilfully avoiding drawing a confrontation out knowing that's what he's trying to do.

'Not having you coming with us,' his voice drops to a deeper rumble. Sarah looks up at him with a loving gaze and gives a small smile. The big man hesitates just for a split second but it's enough to show her he's lost the battle of wills.

'How do you want to do this?' Sergeant Hopewell asks in a business-like manner.

'Do this?' I can feel my temper starting to fray, 'do this? Have you any idea what you're going into. We've been fighting alongside each other solidly for nine days now and we've learnt to move together, to anticipate each other's movements, we know instinctively when to press forward and when to drop back, we've learnt that through nine fucking days of solid fucking fighting so forgive me but it'll be us fucking doing this. You,' I point at them, 'will just get in the fucking way.' Silence for several seconds and stupidly I feel maybe I've gone too far and caused serious offence, still clinging onto cultural values and the strict moral codes of our society. But even more stupidly I press on, ramming the point home, 'I get it…we all get it okay. We get your point that it's not our job to save you and it's not our job to go and die for anyone but…and please listen to this…we stand a better chance of surviving if it is just us…'

'But…' Terri goes to speak but a hard look from me silences her. 'No buts Terri,' I continue with my ranting, 'and they still need someone to look out for them, who is going to do that if we're all dead? What if they get off the boats on the other side and find another horde waiting for them? How are they going to get to the fort or shall we just call Chris and get him to come pick them up in his fleet of coaches?'

'Howie,' Sarah says softly.

'No Sarah, *if* you had been fighting them for the length of time we had and *if* those terrified women and children had someone else to look after them then maybe it would be a good idea but you didn't and they don't so it's a shit idea.'

'How do we get experience if we don't start fighting them Mr Howie?' Tom asks quietly showing a rare serious side to his nature.

'Exactly,' Sarah glares at me, 'and by fighting with you we're taking away the biggest threat which is Darren, and another thing, those women are not some incapable bunch of weaklings. They need to take responsibility for their own safety and they can fire shotguns and swing axes as well as anyone. Stop being so fucking sexist.'

'This isn't about being sexist; this isn't a workplace, this isn't some job where you can moan about equal rights or lack of fucking promotion for women. This is about having the right people to do the task at hand and right now we,' I wave my hand at the men standing by me, 'are the right people to do this simply because we've been doing it non-stop since this thing started.'

'And we won't get experienced and as good as you unless we jump in and start fighting too.' Terri yells back.

'Listen to me and listen well,' I step forward and can feel pure fury threatening to explode. Every word I say comes out through gritted teeth and the rage that propelled me through so many fights and battles suddenly manifests itself making every one of them recoil, 'this is how it is; we are going to head them off and you are going to take our people back to our fort. Do I make myself clear? I SAID DO I MAKE MYSELF CLEAR?' I look to each one in turn, eyes drop away from my intense glare, feet shuffle awkwardly but the silence tells me I've finally got through.

'Okay,' Sarah finally breaks the silence with a quiet response, 'you're right, you've got us this far.'

'We need to get our people inside. Dave, Dean was going to get us some weapons. Find him and tell him we don't need them but take whatever ammunition you can find.'

'On it,' Dave affirms jogging away quickly with Lani running after him.

'Nick, Cookey make sure all our bags have got water and food, Blowers and Clarence I want you two to clean our weapons and make sure they're ready, distribute the ammunition amongst the bags once Dave brings it back.' They break away instantly leaving me with the rest of our group standing in an awkward silence.

'Howie I want you to take Steven and Tom with you, no hang on please let me finish,' Sergeant Hopewell holds her hand up, 'they're good lads, young and fit and they'll keep up. You do understand that while we accept your leadership at this time I am still a Police Sergeant and therefore recognised by any form of government to take control in times of extreme incidents. This is my decision and you will offend me greatly, and these two, if you don't accept them into your group. They are both trained to take orders and they will do as they are told when they are told. The rest of us can ensure the safety of everyone else.'

'Howie listen to the Sergeant,' Ted adds in his fatherly tone, 'you boys know what you're doing out there and we accept that but these lads are itching to get stuck in and like they said, they need the experience and there's no time like the present.' I look at Steven and Tom, my only experiences have been of them squabbling and playing the fool but they're the same age as Nick, Blowers and Cookey and I guess maybe there is a time to be a stubborn fool and a time to concede.

'Okay, lads go and find Dave, get your shotguns sawn off and ask Dave to find you some hand weapons to fight with for when it starts getting nasty. Wait!' I shout as they start running off, 'make sure you have backpacks that the shotguns can fit into, we'll need to be light on our feet and we cannot afford to be holding two weapons if we get caught out.'

'Sir,' they both shout back and start jogging off towards the doors. I can see Terri is seething from the decision made by her Sergeant but Sarah just looks crestfallen and deeply worried. The local guards start moving into the park ushering people back inside. The parents respond instantly with the conception that men with guns must be making the right decisions. Children cry with disappointment as they're pulled and carried away from the play area.

We stroll over to the bags as Clarence and Blowers sit down quickly breaking the shotguns open and cleaning them through. I go from bag to bag taking all the shotgun cartridges out and putting them into a pile, Sarah drops down and starts helping me in stilted silence.

'We don't have enough pistols for Steven and Tom,' I scratch my head already worrying about the smaller details that I know will keep us alive.

'They can have mine and Dave's,' Clarence replies. 'You two are the best shots with them. It'd make more sense for me and one of the others to go without.'

'True, but we're also less likely to need them,' Clarence glances up with a wicked grin breaking the tension with his barbed joke.

'Funny bugger,' I mutter with a quiet laugh.

'Fuck it, I'll take two if you're going to argue,' Cookey jokes, 'I can be like Bruce Willis and dive across the ground firing both of them at the same time.'

'And break your ribs and lie on the floor groaning like a twat,' Blowers adds.

'Oh you'd like me lying on the floor groaning wouldn't you, face down by any chance?' Cookey replies.

'That's what your mum said,' Blowers laughs.
'Don't start on my mum.'
'Well don't start with the gay jokes then.'
'I'm not…I just think it's about time you came out the closet.'
'Your mum wouldn't even fit in the closet.
The lads banter, Clarence smiles and the world rolls on its gentle course as seconds pass into minutes. Before too long the shotguns are cleaned and ready and the cartridges are re-distributed evenly throughout the bags. The lads stand up passing cigarettes round and we enjoy a smoke in the warm summer air, while we wait for Dave to come back.
 So we can move out and pick another fight with a horde of zombies.

Chapter Six

The next few hours are spent working our way further into the town, going from street to street and finding survivors everywhere. It surprises me that these fuckwits don't all get together and fortify one of their shitty little streets. We'd still get through eventually but they would kill a few of us in the process and at least they would go out fighting instead of cowering under their beds covered in their own piss and shit. These fucking pussies are just waiting to die, hiding in vain and convincing each other that help is coming and they just have to wait it out. Slaughtering them becomes so easy that if it wasn't for the sheer frenzied urge of ripping their flesh apart it could almost become boring, I say almost because the urge is so strong that it could never actually become mundane. We get the tactic down to a fine art; entering the street quietly and going to the first house. Breaking a window or simply sending a few heavy zombie bodies at it and smashing it open then I let them rip, sending them in fast and loud and after that we just have to follow the scent of fear until we root them out to finish them off screaming and wailing, begging for the lives. But they don't know what life is until they've tried this. A strange thing happened late in the afternoon which I kept to myself. We had entered one of the big suburban houses and I almost puked at the sight of more beige walls and cream carpets, not to mention the black and white artistically framed photographs of the occupants all dressed in black jumpers and smiling unnaturally. I even saw a picture of a pebble, an actual photograph of a fucking pebble on a beach. Further down the hallway I saw another framed picture of the same pebble but this time it was on a picnic table, then another with the pebble poised artfully next to a stream. What fucking moron took a pebble with them and took pictures of it in different scenes? Fucking arseholes. We found the occupants hiding as normal in the upstairs bedroom. And as normal the mother took a flying charge with a big knife but she got dispatched quickly by Marcy. She was quite fit and attractive and I stood there for a couple of minutes watching her bleed out while Marcy and some of our babies went into the room to finish the screaming brats off. While I was standing there I heard a whimpering coming from another door, following the sound I found an adult male with a thick bushy dark beard hiding behind the shower curtain in the bathroom.

As I pulled the curtain back he pissed himself with fear making me shake my head at his lack of bravery. I told him to kneel down which he did willingly, now if a deranged naked zombie walked into my bathroom and told me to kneel down I'd be telling him to fuck off and throwing everything in sight at his zombie face, but this pussy just complied weakly and knelt down in the bathtub crying his eyes out.

'I'm going to bite you to death,' I said to him but he just stayed there whimpering, 'I'm going to bend down and sink my teeth into your neck and my infection will enter your bloodstream, you will die and a couple of minutes later you'll come back and be one of them stupid twats running around and drooling.'

He still didn't react so I took it slow, bending over and nuzzling his exposed neck with my teeth. The fucker actually craned his head so I could get easier access which just annoyed me so I finished him off quickly with a big bite and watched with interest as he bled out spraying crimson all over the white tiles, like something from a Hitchcock film. With the same detached interest I stood there waiting for him to come back. Eventually he started twitching and convulsing until his eyes opened all red and bloodshot. The funny thing was that I didn't feel a connection to him, there was nothing. I probed and concentrated but he just didn't exist in my mind.

'Wow, this feels strange,' he said in a very normal way.

'You can talk?' I asked him.

'It would appear so,' he replied and started shuffling round from his slumped position in the bathtub.

'Is that all my blood?' He asked with interest pointing at the blood dripping down the walls.
'Yes, how can you talk?'
'How on earth should I know, can't they all talk?'
'No.'
'Well you appear to be talking well enough.'
'That's because I'm special.'
'That woman can talk too, I heard you both.'
'She's special too.'
'Well I guess I must be special too then, here give me a hand.' I didn't like the way he said it as he stretched his arm out. He looked intelligent and cultured, refined and intellectual.
'Well don't just stand there my boy, help me out.'
'My boy?'
'I am decidedly older than you so my use of the phrase "my boy" is inherently one of the deepest respect young man so please don't just stand there, this blood is very slippery.' I stood there watching him slip and slide with growing frustration until he eventually got a grip and stood up properly. He then stepped out of the bath and stood in front of me, examining my face and looking down at my naked body with a slight sneer.
'Why are you naked?'
'Why not?'
'Don't be surly, I asked you a question.'
'You shouldn't speak to me like that.'
'And why not?'
'Because I'm in charge.'

The Undead Day Nine

'Well we shall see about that young man, now I am very hungry and I want you to show me how all this works.'

'Darren who are you talking to?' Marcy called out from behind the bathroom door.

'Just myself, chattering away to myself...' She pushed the door open and walked in to see me standing over the now properly dead man pulling the toothbrush out of his eye socket where I had slammed it in through to the brain.

'What happened to him?'

'Oh he got a bit chopsy so I had to finish him off properly...'

'He's not coming back then?'

'Er...no my love, not this one.'

'Oh well, missing one won't hurt, here I found these for you.' She hands me a pair of blue jeans and in my shocked state of having found not only a talking zombie, but one that clearly wanted to usurp me, take Marcy for himself and rule my babies, I took the jeans with just a smile and a nod.

'Are you okay?' She looked at me quizzically.

'Yep, fine....I'll er...get these on then shall I?' She watched me slip the shoes off and slide the jeans over my legs before bending to put the black office shoes back on. She coughed once and I looked up to see her holding a pair of brown desert boots in her hand.

'You can't wear jeans with office shoes.'

'Why not?'

'They don't go, you'd look awful.'
'Does it matter?'
'Yes it matters now put these on. I won't be seen dead with you dressed like that.'
'But you are dead…we both are.'
'That's not the point and don't be surly.'
'That's what he said…'
'What?'
'Nothing, pass them here then.' The boots get pulled on and I start doing the laces up to the top of the high eyelets.
'No, leave them a bit loose so the jeans tuck into the boots slightly…here like this,' she bent down and fidgeted with them for a few seconds and seeing as she was naked I got a cracking good view of her cherry shaped arse sticking out, 'like that, wow you look good…no you really look good like that with your top off.'
'I feel stupid.'
'No you look so sexy, all rough and nasty,' she purred coming in close to run her hands over my chest. 'Oh you nasty zombie….coming to bite my neck and do bad things to me.' She craned her head back exposing her neck which reminded me off the chatty beardy man at my feet with a bright pink toothbrush sticking out his eye. Even so, the sight of her neck set something off in me and I bit down, not hard but enough to draw a little blood which got her going straight away, digging her nails into

my back and raking down hard enough to rip the flesh open.

The same erotic feeling I had when she first turned flooded through me and I gripped her harder, licking at the blood dripping down her neck. She in turn bit me on the shoulder and started probing her hot tongue into the wound, licking at the salty infected blood and sucking away. My hands groped round to her butt. My fingers brushing over the dried scab on the congealed wound. I started picking away at it, gently at first then harder and harder, prising the dried claret away and exposing the still unhealed flesh beneath. Groaning in ecstasy she bit me again which set me off more. Then she got inventive and unbuckled my jeans to pull them down round my ankles, she pushed me down onto the toilet seat and straddled me, impaling herself on my now hardened dead member. With continual biting, tearing and ripping of each other's flesh we made love on a dirty toilet seat in a stranger's house with a dead zombie watching us with one eye and a toothbrush sticking out his skull, not to mention the several members of our horde standing patiently on the landing drooling away while watching our noisy love making.

Now, outside and wearing my stupid jeans tucked into the tops of the stupid boots and feeling like some stupid zombie catalogue poser I'm looking back down the street and examining the densely packed undead babies all staring forward at me and Marcy. The whole of the street is crammed with them, from one side to the other and back as far as I can see there are dead faces drooling and staring with red bloodshot eyes. The connection is strong and I suddenly stride forward marching at them. They obey to the will of my mind instantly and scuttle back to form a narrow path down the middle. Within a couple of seconds they are standing to attention in neat lines, perfectly spaced and staring dead ahead like the lovely little soldiers they are. Marcy and I walk down the middle, examining them and noting the ones with the worse injuries.

'They can go in the first wave; we'll keep the stronger ones back,' Marcy says and I send the instruction out through the hundreds of strands of telepathic connectors that entwine us all. Instructing and marking them as first group or second.

'Actually,' Marcy pauses, 'we'll do it in stages and send in the most injured first, then the next lot with not so bad injuries, then the ones with slight injuries and the strongest healthiest and freshest we'll keep with us until the end. No point in wasting the good ones at the start...we'll let the weaker ones break down their defences and learn where the weak links are.'

'But I've already started telling them to go in two stages.'

'Then we'll go back to the beginning and start again,' she smiles about turns and starts wiggling her naked behind back to the end of the line. Grumbling and muttering to myself I follow her and watch as she starts examining them again but closer this time.

'Can you make them present their injuries so we don't have to keep looking for them?'

'For fuck's sake this is fucking stupid the poor cunts shouldn't have to stand there parading their wounds.'

'Darren, just do it please,' she snaps. The zombies are a sudden hive of activity as they shuffle and twist round, bending, kneeling, lifting tops up or dropping trousers to show their cuts, bites, lacerations and gouges.

'That's better, thank you…now how about we number them into groups, say four groups? I'll give them a number and you tell them what group they're in.'

'This isn't a fucking school sports day Marcy.'

'Are the men and women of the same strength and ferocity?' She ignores my sarcasm.

'Yep pretty much, the bigger ones move a bit slower but obviously their extra weight helps them at the end. Also, moving them too fast in the daytime weakens them.'

'By how much?'

'It depends; if they've been dead a while then they'll weaken faster because of the rate of decomposition they've already suffered. The fresher ones should last longer…'

'We shall move them at a steady pace and keep them conserved until we need them to start shifting, right I'll count out and you tell them what group they're in.

'This is fucking stupid…why don't we just go now and rip Howie's fucking face off, we've got loads and most of them are fresh.'

'Did that work the last time Darren? No…so please just do as I ask.'

'Fine!'

'One…Four…Three…Four…'

'Slow down, I can't keep up.'

'Darren this isn't rocket science …'

'Just slow down.'

'Where did you get to?'

'I don't know, start again.'

'Darren!'

'Sorry love but you went too fast, just do it slower.'

'One….got it?'

'Yes.'

'Four…got it?'

'Don't take the piss.'

'Well apparently you couldn't keep up a minute ago…'

'Just fucking count them out,' I shout in anger, she flashes a mean look at me before turning away dramatically and reeling the numbers off.

Following behind her I send the messages as we go

and let them stand easy once they've been checked and counted. The poor things shuffle and relax behind us as we work our way down the long lines with Marcy examining wounds like some field doctor and shouting numbers out.

'Ooh, what about this one?' She asks after a few minutes.

'He's only got one arm Marcy.'

'Yeah I know but he looks strong and healthy though.'

'Yeah for a one armed zombie...'

'We'll put him in the third group...I think he'll do well.'

'The third? Are you joking? He needs to go in one or two.'

'But look at the muscles in his good arm.'

'What do you mean his good arm? He doesn't have a good arm, he has one arm.'

'Stop being pedantic Darren, three please.'

'Okay,' telepathically I tell him he's a two and hope Marcy doesn't notice later, I'll just blame it on the confusion of battle.

We keep going down the lines, reaching a junction and sweeping round to the left and even I'm surprised at how many we've taken in just one day. Standing on the junction I look up then off to the left and the sheer sight of the hundreds and hundreds of zombies makes me grin like the demented super zombie I am. Fuck you Dave you cuntrunt, try swinging your penknives at this lot and see where it gets you. Mind you he is good though, the nasty little prick is too good really. I fucking hate the way he leaps about like some fucked up ballet dancer. What fucking right has he got to be that good, it isn't fucking fair that he's on their side, why can't we have a Dave on our side. Fuck it, I'll just send all of them after Dave and get him turned. Ha, Howie would be royally fucked up the arse then if we sent zombie Dave after him. But then Dave would see it coming and probably stab himself in the brain to make sure he wouldn't come back. Fucking stupid cuntrunt stabbing himself in the brain, that's not fucking fair, it's fucking cheating is what it is.

'Darren!'

'What?'

'You're ranting…'

'Oh am I? Sorry, just thinking about Dave stabbing himself in the brain.'

'What? Why would he do that?'

'Because he's a prize cunt is why, it's the sort of stupid cheating fucked up thing he would do, just so he wouldn't have to go after his fucking limp wristed cock sucking boyfriend Howie.'

'Darren!'

'What?'

'You're ranting again, can we just get on with it…and don't be homophobic.'

'What!?'

'I don't like it, my brother was gay.'

'Marcy if you saw your brother standing there now you would eat his brains.'
'That's not the point, don't use gay things in your ranting.'
'How about racism? Can I use that?'
'No!'
'Oh so just generalised non-specific abusive ranting then?'
'Four…Two…Two…One…' She presses on before I start off on one again.
'How about people with learning difficulties? Can I take the piss out of them?'
'No…my cousin was in a wheelchair…Three….Two….Four…'
'That's disabled not learning difficulties.'
'Well he was a bit retarded too…Three…One…One.'
'You can't say retarded anymore.'
'What? Who said so?'
'If I can't call Howie a gay cunt then you can't call people retards.'
'Fine…One…One…One…there's a lot of ones here.'
'There not ours Marcy, they were already turned and I've got no connection to them.'
'Oh that's a shame, he wasn't really retarded he was just a bit thick really…Three…Two…'
'If you saw a person with learning difficulties would you bite them?'
'Darren we have spent the day slaughtering every living person we've come across and a few of them did have learning difficulties.'

'Did they? I didn't notice any.'
'They were killed before you got there; you just sucked on them a bit.'
'…I didn't notice any difference in the taste.'
'One…Three…Three…Two…'

Chapter Seven

We head back down the narrow path, trudging through the shaded trees and back out beside the high wall that looks out along the sweep of the bay towards the town. Clarence, Dave, Blowers, Nick, Cookey and I along with Steven and Tom. Leaving was hard on all of us, not just our group but the people left behind. Again. We had more arguments from Sarah and Terri which at one point threatened to spiral out of control until Ted and Sergeant Hopewell stepped in using their vast policing experience to calm everyone down. Thankfully Steven and Tom had the sense to stay quiet and not get drawn in, I think they were worried that if they got involved they could end up staying and miss the opportunity to come with us. Personally, if I was in their shoes I would have jumped at the chance of staying in the relative safety of the bunkers while some crazy idiots went off to charge a load of frenzied undead, especially with nightfall only a couple of hours away. But then that's wrong because I could stay there if I wanted to. Any of us could. We could easily argue that we've done enough and just refuse to leave. I'm not sure that if it came to it we would be forced out at gunpoint, we have weapons too and everyone in there could see we're experienced with them. So no, I wouldn't have stayed if I was in their shoes. I haven't "stayed" since this thing began.

Some of Sarah's words resonate through my mind as we walk in silence. She said again that we're getting addicted to it, that the killing is something we enjoy instead of it being a necessity only to be done when absolutely necessary. I could tell that comment made us all feel a little uncomfortable and maybe there is some truth in it. If we thought it through and really contemplated it seriously we could probably come up with another way of leaving without having to fight. We could have considered taking our group further along the coast until we found another harbour with boats. This Island must have loads of harbours. With the retired navy captain with us we could have probably made our way to one of the commercial ports that the tourist ferries use and taken everyone away together.

So why choose this option then? Glancing round I can see that all of us, apart from Steven and Tom, have serious intent expressions. We know what is coming and how truly awful it will be. We know that the simplest of mistakes could mean the death of us all. No machine guns, no safety of the Saxon APC and with two new untrained and inexperienced fighters we are virtually offering ourselves as a sacrifice, Terri said as much in her final attempt at getting us to change our minds and either stay or take them with us.

But it isn't that. It is something else. Our race has been challenged and as a result we have seen our families, friends and comrades die horrible, brutal and violent deaths. Something in us will simply not accept that. It's wrong and it has to be challenged because the consequences are simply too utterly terrifying to contemplate. Bad things happen when good people stand by and do nothing. Darren was one of us and it's almost as though he chose to be on their side. He could have gone off somewhere else and been a zombie. He didn't have to come after us the way he did and he wilfully took the lives of our loved ones. Sarah is close when she says it's an addiction we've got used to. It isn't that, it's the chance to take back what is ours by right of virtue. It's the chance to make a decision as free men and see it through. To show them we will not cower and hide. And maybe a small part of it is the prospect of battle, standing in line next to your mate and culling the evil spawn of the devil sent at us. Virtuous. Glorious. Righteous.

In the end it was Clarence and Dave that gave their pistols up to Tom and Steven. Taking them aside for a few minutes and drilling them with dry firing, re-loading and more dry-firing. Again I was surprised at how the two lads responded seriously and didn't piss about and squabble like they do most of the time. But then I caught Ted glaring at them and figured he'd had a quiet and most likely very threatening word with them to behave. They look the part now with similar backpacks strapped on and sawn off shotguns wedged in so the stocks poke out. Pistols are strapped on the police utility belts they still wear, and I notice that Tom still carries his Taser and extendable baton. Dave even managed to find them an axe each, not as large as the ones we looted from the DIY store but more like the first one I started out with. They just don't look hardened like the other lads. There is fear and nervous energy in their faces. Not just fear of what's coming but also that they don't look stupid in front of the rest of us.

'Lads listen up, if and when it starts getting horrible I want you to split up and stick with Clarence and Dave. Keep your ears open and listen for the instructions given. Not just from me but from all of us. Clarence and Dave are both extremely experienced so don't try and copy them or do what they do. Do not over-extend or allow yourselves to get isolated or trapped. Aim for the head and keep moving. The shotguns have incredible fire power but the range is shit. Remember that.'

'What do we do if we get trapped or surrounded?' Tom asks.

'Fight like bastards,' Blowers replies quickly, they both grin at the quick answer but the smiles soon vanish when they see he's not joking.

'Is that Lani?' Nick cuts in pointing across to a wooden bench set against the wall where a small figure sits watching the sea, a backpack rests by her feet and a huge meat cleaver is across her lap.

She turns her head to watch us approaching; her face stays impassive and expressionless.
'Lani,' I nod as we gather round the bench.
'Mr Howie,' she nods back and stares at me defiantly.
'Why are you out here?'
'I'm coming with you,' she stands quickly and starts shrugging the backpack on.
'Still got my gun then?' I notice the stock poking out the top of the bag.
'Nope, I got another one. I put yours back in your bag.'
'Nice meat cleaver Lani,' Nick grins genuinely pleased to see her again.
'Lani...'
'Mr Howie,' she cuts me off, 'I'm coming with you. It's my family out there, it's those zombies that took my family, friends and everyone I've ever known or cared about. This is my choice. I waited here for you so it didn't make it awkward for you in there,' she nods back towards the fort, 'but this is my choice, my decision.' She reaches down to pick the meat cleaver up from the bench and stands ready and waiting. Looking down I see she's even found a pair of boots instead of the trainers she was wearing before.
'Lani, please go back and wait with the others.'
'No. I'm coming with you. I've killed a few of them and I survived for nine days on my own so I've earned my place.'

'I know you did Lani but I'd still rather you waited here.'
'Why because I'm a girl?'
'No it's not that.'
'Mr Howie I'm not going back. I respect you're in charge and I will follow your orders exactly, I won't slow you down or get in the way and this is the only time I'll be rude to you but with all due respect Sir you can fuck off if you think you can make me stay.' The way she says it, so polite yet firm makes me burst out laughing. Not in a take the piss kind of way, and she can see I'm not patronising her. She just won the point and she knows it, glancing round with a wry smile and a glint in her eye that reminds me of Dave.
'Bloody hell are you two related by any chance?' looking between them both I shake my head at the similarities.
'No Mr Howie, I think Lani is from Thailand,' Dave replies seriously.
'Right well let's get going then,' I sigh at the sheer absurdity of it and hear Nick give an audible "Yes!" which gets quick glances from the rest of us. With Nick looking sheepish we move out and on this ninth day we become nine. Nine bloody idiots going out to pick a fight with a dirty bunch of infected zombies.
Still, at least it's not raining.

Chapter Eight

'What's it called again?'
'Puckpool,' she answers.
'That's a stupid fucking name for a place. You think that's where they've gone?'
'It's the only place round here that could hold that many people, we'll try there first,' she says and having clearly made the decision of where we're going she strides on. Marcy also decided that it wasn't appropriate to go into battle naked, I argued this by saying that it might distract some of the young lads if she comes charging at them with her boobs bouncing about all over the place. I got a funny look for that comment and she asked me if I thought her boobs were saggy then. I said no of course I didn't think that but any woman's boobs would bounce if she ran about naked. Dressed to kill, I'm still wearing the fucking awful jeans and boots. She noticed that I pulled the bottoms of the jeans out from the boots and refused to walk anywhere until I'd tucked them back in. In just this one day I've learnt that doing what Marcy wants makes my undead life a lot easier. She's very bossy but then she does keep reminding me of how I screwed up before when I had tens of thousands of zombies with me, and anyone that can fuck something like that up needs to be told what to do. I've never really had a girlfriend before. In the previous life I was just a lazy twat that smoked too

much dope and hung around on the streets doing fuck all. That and playing Xbox was pretty much all I did. Then they told me I had to join the Territorial Army to get my benefit money. Stupid fuckers should have left me at home smoking weed and playing Call of Duty. So I've never really had a girlfriend before or even that much to do with women so I don't know if they're all this bossy and demanding. But she's very pretty and she seems to know what she's doing so it's easier to just go along with it, and a super zombie should have a good woman with him.

Finally she was ready after pissing about making sure her clothes were right and her hair was brushed and the blood was washed from her face. Then she put a little bit of make up on while me and the horde stood about making small talk. Well I made small talk and they just listened mostly, with the odd sympathetic groan here and there. When she came out of the house she was using I had my babies doing some warm up exercises, stretching their arms back and forth and a bit of light jogging on the spot. They were already formed up in their four groups so the ones nearest to me were the worst of the bunch with ragged injuries and limbs half hanging off. The ones that hadn't been turned by me were just standing there staring dumbly with drool pouring out of their mouths.

Marcy led us through the streets, going pretty much back the way we came, all the better to admire the trail of destruction we'd left behind us. Doors hanging open, windows smashed in, blood smears and trails everywhere and the odd corpse of those that had been too heavily injured or eaten by the horde. As we neared the seafront I could smell the blazing buildings long before they came into sight and turning the last corner before the esplanade I looked back with sheer joy at the huge roaring fire spread along the whole row of buildings from the hotel through to the last house. Long orange flames licked up at the sky as thick black clouds rolled and boiled around them.l Now with the blaze behind us we set off on the road parallel to the sweeping bay, heading towards Howie and his little piggy fucktards.

Chapter Nine

'Lani, once we make contact we need to lead them inland and away from here,' I drop back a few steps with Dave and Clarence to speak with our local expert.

'We need somewhere we can use for the night,' Clarence adds, 'somewhere defensible.'

'What like a house or something?' Lani asks.

'Too many points of entry in a house,' Dave says, 'we want to funnel them so they can't all attack at the same time.'

'But with an escape route in case we have to give ground,' Clarence adds.

'You don't want much then,' she looks thoughtfully ahead, 'there's a big church at the top of the town. It's got a main entrance with double doors and a big porch that sticks out.'

'A recessed door, how big is the recess?' Dave asks.

'I don't know,' she answers with a shake of her head.

'Roughly, how many people could fit in it?'

'About ten in a line from front to back if they were squashed up.'

'Other doors?' Dave probes.

'There's a back entrance that goes into an annexe, they use it for first aid training and that kind of thing. There's a door that leads from the annexe into the church but it's really old and solid.'

'Single or double sized?' Dave continues.

'Erm, it's only a single door.'
'What about the windows?
'They're glass but they're quite high up and narrow. It's got a big spire that people can go up to look down at the town.'
'That would be perfect if we had rifles instead of shotguns, are there any gunsmiths in the town?' I ask her.
'Any what?' She asks.
'Gunsmiths, shops that sell guns.'
'No, only in the main town about ten miles away.'
'So it's got a main recessed entrance and the rear door, any other exits?' I ask.
'There might be but I only know those two.'
'A church has thick walls and it would funnel them with a deep porch, but if there's only two exits we could get trapped,' Clarence says.
'But with that tower Lani mentioned we could go up that and hold them off easily, that will only have a single access point or stairs that could be defended. It's a strong contender, what other places are there?' I ask again and watch Lani as she looks out to the distance in contemplation.
'The pier?' She points across the bay to the long black pier jutting out into the blue water, 'that's long and thin with only one way up it.'
'How wide is it?' Dave asks.
'Er, maybe two car widths or a bit more than that. I know two cars can pass each other on the way up.'

'That's quite wide, it'll be hard to defend but we'll keep it in mind. I think we should aim for the church unless we find something else on the way or Lani thinks of any other places.' They nod back as I glance round to make sure everyone heard the plan and we keep going. In the distance we can see the huge plumes of thick black smoke high in the air and I get a visual image of Chris standing at the back of the fort looking over the sea and watching the smoke with a small wry smile wondering what devastation we're wreaking over here.

None of has eaten properly or slept for a long time, getting by on adrenalin and adventure. The threat of death has kept us alert and ready but this can't be sustained. At some point we need to stop, rest, eat, sleep but right now I can't think when that will be. Every time we think we've reached our objective things change and fuck up. We had to fight to get the Saxon, then fight to reach the hospital and Sarah. Then we were fighting all the way back down thinking we'll be safe at the forts only to face another massive battle. Each time we keep thinking this will be it, this will be the final act and we can rest but as with everything else since this terrible event started it's all gone to rat shit. Even now marching out we're thinking we'll lure Darren away and get our people back to our fort and then it'll be over but it won't. It will never be over.

We need to evolve the same way Darren is, or the way the infection keeps changing. Something inside me screams that we need to attack and drive them down, press the attack and keep going no matter what happens. Lure them away, fight, run, fight and all the time cull their numbers. Only by killing every last one of them can we ever hope to live in peace. Darren won't stop until he turns every last one of us. He has to die and die properly this time.

Chapter Ten

Howie is a cunt, a dirty cunning bastard and as long as he is alive he will inspire all the other hero wannabes that they can fight and kill us. Instead of hiding away and being easy prey for us to come along and chomp on them, they'll get all tough with nasty gleams in their eyes and instead of standing there pissing themselves and shaking like leaves holding little kitchen knives, they'll be going into their garages and sheds looking for big heavy sharp things. Making weapons and learning how to use bows and arrows. I could arm my babies and give them all knives but the stupid buggers would probably just stab themselves or each other when they got all frenzied and worked up. And there's no way I can control so many individuals if they're using hand weapons. I can lead them, show them which way to go and even control a few during a scrap but that's about it. The control I have is strong but not that good. So before Howie and his cuntrunt Dave can start leading some kind of do-gooding resistance movement he has to die. He has to die painfully and slowly, an awful death that makes him scream and beg and when he turns I'll send him back to them so they have to kill him again. That will take the fight out of them. It will send a message to leave us alone and let us live in peace. We need to feed just the same as them and we've as much right as they do to go after our food

source. Just because it happens to be them we need to eat to survive is not our fault. That's nature. Lions and wolves aren't evil. They kill to survive. They take what they need to ensure the survival of their species. Same as us.
This has to end and Howie must die before he becomes a folk hero cunt with songs sung about him. Poems and stories whispered at night to small children about how they need to eat their vegetables and sleep well so they can grow big and strong and become like Howie the hero of the people. Fuck him. Fuck Dave and Fuck Howie and Fuck all their little piggy fucktard twats.

Chapter Eleven

'Contact Mr Howie, straight ahead of us on the road,' Dave shades his eyes to stare off into the distance. Copying his actions I strain and squint until tears start filling my eyes but I can't see anything. Just the beach, the sea, the woods to one side and the road ahead of us stretching for miles. 'Yeah I can see them,' Blowers says, 'in the distance there's a thick black line of them. They almost look part of the road Mr Howie.' I relax my gaze and stare at the road ahead of us letting my eyes sweep along the concrete, taking in all the details and colours until there in the far distance I see a black smudge that becomes clearer as my mind works to process the images. The smudge is moving. A snake slithering across the road, long, dark and gently undulating.

'There must be hundreds,' I can already feel my heart beating faster at the sight of them. They are earlier than expected. We thought we'd be able to get into the town and find them before they started coming for us. The fact that they're heading in this direction means they've worked out where our group could be hiding.

'There's a lane at the side of the café Mr Howie, where we found the van earlier to pull the shutters off. We can lead them up that lane and away from here,' Lani suggests urgently. Looking down the path I can see the café, then I look further up at the black mass of undead and then back down to the café.

'Speed up,' I give the simple order and start a gentle jog. We need to make that café well before they get close. We need a chance for them to see us, start coming and then leg it away. Checking round me I see the others are moving faster now and thankfully they've sorted their bags well enough that nothing falls out or comes loose. Waiting a couple of minutes for stiff muscles to warm up I gradually increase the pace. Still jogging but getting faster and ensuring we get to that café.

Chapter Twelve

'I spy with my zombie eye something beginning with C.'
'C?' Marcy asks, a puzzled expression on her face.
'Cunts,' I nod forward and point to the distance.
'Can you see them?' She says excitedly, staring off and scanning the bay, beach, sea. Everywhere but the bloody path in front of her.
'See them? I can smell the nasty little wankers.'
'Really?' She sniffs the air in front of her.
'Not literally Marcy.'
'Oh well don't say it then if you can't actually smell them. Is that them?' She points to the distant figures.
'Yep, I'd recognise his gay run anywhere.'
'Darren! What did I say about using gay insults?'
'Sorry Marcy?'
'Thank you.'
'They're coming straight at us.'
'We should speed up,' she says.
'No, don't waste energy. They're coming this way so let them get closer before we do anything.' I can feel his blood in my mouth. I can taste it. I can taste Howie's death. He's close. So is Dave. My undead zombie heart kicks up a notch and despite what I just said I can't help but start moving faster.

Chapter Thirteen

'Quicker,' muscles warmed up and lungs starting to work harder we increase our pace and keep watch between the café and the thick mass coming towards us.

'Everyone okay?' I call out mainly for the benefit of the new arrivals but I get a round robin chorus of replies. Eyes now locked on the horde I can see Darren has been busy killing and gathering more undead to join his evil quest. There are hundreds of them all moving as one and keeping steady with their leader.

Getting closer I can see two distinct figures out front, one of them must be Darren but I have no idea who the other is or how his vanity would allow someone else to walk out front with him.

Our two groups, so vastly different in size edge closer and closer. The gap shrinks with every step we take and every one of those steps brings us closer to the real and serious risk of dying a horrible tortured death at the hands and mouths of those evil spawn.

With the café in full view now we keep running and see there is a safe length of distance between us and them and thankfully the horde have not started running at us yet.

'He's learning,' Dave says.

'He is mate, keeping them full of energy so we can have a good scrap. Hear that lads? Darren is keeping them all safe and together, he's learning, he's getting better.'

'Fuck him Mr Howie,' Blowers snorts.

'We'll still win,' Nick adds and I hear the hard tones in their voices, the bitterness and the rage is there, ready to be focussed and used.

'I fucking love this,' Cookey suddenly spits out making the rest of us laugh, 'why don't we just fucking charge them and get at it.'

Stupidly. Amazingly and without doubt his suggestion gains a second or two of serious thought. Well I know I give it serious thought and something hangs in the air that suggest Dave, Clarence and the other two lads are too. Not so sure about Tom, Steven and Lani though.

'I never told you this before Clarence, but er…Darren once said you were fat and ugly,' Cookey continues the jokes, his way of dealing with the impending fight.

'Did he now?' Clarence growls.

'Do you think they've seen us?' Steven asks. Despite his nervous question his voice sounds steady enough.

'I reckon so mate,' my voice comes out low and gets a quick glance from Dave jogging at my side. He gives a small rare smile and I can see the gleam in his eyes.

'Nick, get in the café and drag out the gas bottles from that barbeque,' Dave orders as we reach the front of the building. The horde are several hundred metres away and still moving at the same steady pace but the sheer size of the zombie army coming at us makes it feel as if they are closer. We pause, chests rising and falling as we get our breathing back under control. Nick darts in, re-appearing with a gas bottle in each hand. Dave takes one from Nick and takes the pistol from Nick's belt all in one smooth move. He hands the gas bottle to Clarence and nods at the approaching horde. Clarence looks down at the gas bottle, takes it and weighs it in his hand for a second while looking at the zombies. With a nod at Dave he turns to face them.

'No fucking way,' Cookey mutters, 'they're too far away.'

'Yeah? Watch this, ready Dave?' Clarence says quietly.

'Ready,' Dave slides the top of the pistol back and stands with it held in a two handed grip down in front of him. Clarence swings the gas bottle back and forth a few times before spinning round and forward and sending it soaring into the sky. Dave's reaction is instant, the pistol is raised and tracks the bottle as it sails slowly end over end towards the horde. The rest of us watch with baited breath as the bottle arcs up then starts coming down to earth; clearing the front of the horde and dropping down deep within the ranks. Two loud retorts sound out. One from the single shot Dave fires and a split second later from the gas bottle as it explodes. The pressure wave sends the packed ranks spewing out in all directions, lacerated by scorching hot fragments of the gas bottle and burnt from the ignition of the gas contained within. Cheers erupt as Clarence is handed the second bottle, he nods at Dave then spins round and forward again. As he releases the bottle he roars out in animalistic rage and the gas bottle flies higher and goes further than the previous one. Dave tracks the bottle and again fires at the very last second; as it drops to within a few feet of the horde. With a huge explosion the bottle bursts into a ball of flame eliciting another eruption of cheers from us.

'Fuck it, that's got them going,' I say as the horde starts running towards us and I just catch a glimpse of some of them stumbling over the bodies of their fallen comrades in death.

'Get going,' there's no need to give that order because we're off. Jogging up the side of the café on the narrow road which starts off as a gentle slope but soon becomes a steep incline and within a couple of minutes I can feel my thighs starting to burn from the exertion.

'Shitting hell,' Nick groans with the same discomfort.

'Stop moaning, it's only a small hill,' Lani smiles at the lads, looking fresh and unflustered she strides easily and clearly has a level of fitness like Dave who is also powering up without issue. The incline

increases and the hill seems to go on forever, draining our legs and sapping vital energy.
Glancing back I can see the front of the horde are nearly at the café with Darren and what looks like a beautiful woman out front.

'Darren's got a girlfriend,' I pant with ragged breath.

'Has he?' Blowers, Nick and Cookey all twist round to look, 'she looks crumpet,' Blowers smirks.

'FUCK YOU SMITHY,' Cookey bellows as he sticks two fingers up. Blowers and Nick repeat the act and I turn back to see Darren running with one hand up, extending his middle finger in our direction.

'Does this hill ever end,' Nick grumbles again after a few more seconds of constant running.

'Not far,' Lani replies. We trudge up, one foot in front of the other, chests heaving and muscles straining with exertion. None of us slow down though. If we stop now we won't be able to get going again.

'Dig in,' Clarence encourages the others, desperately willing them on despite the pain and agony, 'keep going, not far now,' I can see he is suffering. Maybe more than us as his thigh muscles are massive and a man of his size is not designed for rapid stamina work like this.

Groans, growls, moans sound out between us as the bastard hill just keeps going. 'Don't worry about

them,' Clarence catches Steven glancing round, his face red and sweating freely, 'just keep moving.' 'Give it here,' Dave drops back to take the axe from Nick who is clearly struggling and I watch Lani discretely moving to take the same from Cookey. He gives it up with barely a response. Dave and Lani run easily, each holding two heavy hand weapons while the rest of us feel the vomit rising in our stomachs and throats.
'Almost there,' Lani points up ahead with the giant meat cleaver which barely trembles in her grasp. Dave glances across at Lani and he looks as devoid of expression as normal I can tell from the constant time we've spent in each other's company that he's impressed. The hill continues to rise as the car park they took the van from drops further and further behind. If Lani thinks we can make it to the top she must be crazy. Then I see it. A small entrance on the right leading into a narrow lane. The sight of the lane gives us a final burst of speed and we reach it with our lungs gasping for more air and our legs feeling like lead. Turning into the lane I notice it's bordered on one side by a thicket of dense trees and on the other by a high wire fence. The sudden relief of not having to power against gravity is amazing and we half run half hobble into the lane that's only wide enough for two abreast. I drop back with Dave and Clarence and urge the rest past me, eventually bringing up the rear with Clarence at my side and Dave behind us.

The lane twists through the trees following the high wire fence that soon gives way to a high brick wall.

'Here,' Lani shouts and stops, pointing up at the wall, 'go over here.'

'Why?' I shout from the back.

'The wall has broken glass all along the top apart from this bit here; we can go through the grounds of the nunnery and come out further along.'

'Do it, quick get over,' I shout forward and watch Clarence push the rest out of the way to reach the front. Dropping his axe he grasps Lani round the waist and launches her on to the top of the wall with ease before twisting round to grab and hoist the next one up. With Clarence throwing people, the lads scrabbling up and Dave leaping like a gazelle we get over the wall and slump down getting our breath for a few seconds.

'Shotguns…get them ready,' I gasp and stagger backwards a few steps to make sure the horde can see us through the wire fencing. I reach back and draw mine out as the front of the horde comes into view. They're undead zombies but even they are blowing out their arses at having to charge up that bloody hill. Darren and the woman are out in front, he slows down and we lock eyes for a few seconds. On seeing me he surges forward only to be grabbed and pulled back by the woman, he turns and says something to her but she yells and pulls him back just as the horde surge past him, giving safety to them with their bodies.

'YOU LOOK LIKE A TWAT IN THOSE JEANS DARREN,' Cookey bellows to sniggers from Nick and Blowers. Tom and Steven exchange nervous glances as they hold their shotguns ready.

'FUCK YOU COOKEY I'M GOING TO EAT YOUR FUCKING FACE OFF,' Darren screams out from somewhere in the midst of his horde who are all trying to squeeze down the narrow lane.

'THAT WOMAN IS FIT DARREN WHAT'S SHE DOING WITH YOU?' Blowers yells out, 'SEND HER OVER FIRST SHE LOOKS NICE.'

'Get a few now,' I step towards the fence and fire both barrels into the densely packed horde the other side. Loud metallic twangs sound out as the pellets strike the fence but the damage to the zombies is awesome. A second or two later and eight more shotguns fire two barrels each and we watch with unabated glee as they start dropping from the fire.

'COMING OVER,' Dave shouts a warning as the first of the horde gains the top of the wall and drops down on our side. Lani darts forward almost as quick as Dave and I watch Dave hold back at the last second and let Lani swing the cleaver round, taking the zombies head clean off its shoulders. Re-loaded we fire again into the horde as Dave yells to start moving back.

The zombies spread further down the wall climbing onto the broken glass and dropping down with blood pumping from fresh cuts and fingers hanging off from the sharp shards.
Dropping back steadily we re-load and help each other to shove the shotguns back into bags and I quickly glimpse the flush of excitement on Tom and Steven's faces from what could be their first kills. The grounds slope down to a large detached house and we start jogging to gain distance as the undead breach the walls en masse. The wire fencing begins to buckle as the horde start powering against it in a synchronised effort that must be the work of Darren controlling them.
'Fuck it's a zombie nun!' Cookey yells out with alarm. A black and white robed figure staggers into view from the side of the building. More follow until there's a line of black and white penguin-like zombie nuns.
'I'm not killing a nun,' Blowers shouts.
'It's not a nun,' I shout back.
'Sorry Mr Howie but I can't kill a nun.'
'This way,' Lani steers us off to the left away from the undead nuns, weaving through a collection of outbuildings and down a driveway to a set of gates that hang open. Large dried stains of blood spatter the ground, smearing the approach to the big house.

'Don't take us back up the hill,' Nick pleads as we burst out into a quiet residential street to see the same evil incline rising off to the left.
'Okay just for you,' With a smile Lani leads us down the hill and cuts down an alley at the side of another big house. We run through perfectly manicured lawns and trample flower beds as we climb low fences and break through to a main road, again on a bloody great big hill and facing more large Victorian houses.
'Every bloody street looks the same in this shitty town,' Blowers growls looking up and down the hill. Thankfully Lani leads us down the hill this time back towards the seafront having taken us in a big loop. Still jogging but with a steadier pace we're all sweating and flushed, apart from the two weird fitness freaks among us. As we near a junction at the bottom of the road the horde start bursting out of the gardens we've just come through, staggering into the road and hardly breaking stride as they continue their hunting.
'Oh my god Mr Howie!' Cookey yells out, standing still with a terrified expression on his face. He puts his fist to his mouth and turns back quickly to glance at the horde coming after us. 'I think we're being chased by zombies!' the stance he adopts with the mock expression of terror sets us off and we burst out laughing. Grinning like an idiot Cookey starts jogging again. Knackered, breathing hard, sweating, armed to the teeth and being

chased by several hundred zombie creatures we crack up laughing as we run. Giggles of mirth sound out and I know it's just the nervous excitement manifesting but it still feels good to be laughing. A little surreal but good.

Turning into the junction Lani continues to lead us down quiet side streets and it's not long before we start to see signs of the devastation that Darren has wrought, bringing our laughing and frivolity to an abrupt end and reminding us of how much death and suffering must have taken place just hours before. Windows and doors smashed, bodies strewn everywhere. Some are old and already decomposing, festering in the hot summer sun and writhing with the bloated fat white bodies of maggots. Some are fresh kills still with glistening injuries that hardly look human due to the amount of flesh eaten away. Entrails, organs and limbs have been hacked apart. The sour, metallic tang of filth, blood and rancid half cooked meat fills the air mixing with the smoky scent from the fires still raging nearby like the aftermath of some macabre barbeque.

Our pace stays steady, we keep the horde a few hundred metres behind us and I only wish we had greater fire power to whittle them down as we run. The Saxon and the GPMG would make short work of this bunch and it makes me think that without weapons like that and the people that know how to utilise them this ongoing battle could be long and

drawn out if we're reduced to using things like shotguns and axes.
Breathing gets harder and the dull aches in our legs spread as we power on. Dave orders everyone to draw water from their bags and to sip it down as we jog but not to gulp it too quickly. Helping each other we take the bottles out, squirting the gloriously cool liquid onto our faces to rinse the stinging sweat from our eyes. Even Lani is starting to look a little red in the cheeks and her beautiful silky black hair starts to stick to her glistening forehead. Tom and Steven both keep pace and look neither fresher nor more knackered than the rest.
'We have to go back uphill but we can stagger it using side streets,' Lani says her voice still strong and confident. She jogs just ahead of me and I watch her lithe athletic body running with so much grace she's like water running down a stream. Each movement is precise but relaxed, no energy wasted, her arms stay relatively still and don't pump away, her head stays relaxed and sways gently as she bobs along, her feet come up enough to propel her along and no more. So much like Dave and I wonder how people are made so differently. Clarence with his enormous strength and huge heart must be suffering more than any of us having to carry his weight along. He doesn't moan once and I know that so many years in the forces must have left him with more stamina than a big guy like him would normally have. His face is

set, serious and focussed. All our faces are as we start to climb another hill and have to internally change to a lower gear to keep the momentum going.

'Keep going, it's not far,' Lani urges us on, dropping back and speaking in low tones to some of the lads, offering to take their axes but I see their stubborn pride showing and they refuse.

'Go right Mr Howie,' Lani points to another junction further up the hill and again we dig in and drive on desperate to reach the flat street. As we turn I feel a sense of victory, the worst of the pain eases off as the ground levels out and I call out encouraging everyone to keep moving and not slow down.

'They've gained a little distance,' Dave says loud enough for us all to hear, 'don't speed up lads, keep this pace,' Dave adds at the burst of power applied at his bad news, sounding more like a drill sergeant than ever before.

More houses with shattered doors. More broken windows. More blood. More devastation as we go deeper into this town following the route that Darren took on his quest for food. Our lives are so entwined now and I can sense him behind us, the infection or disease or whatever dirty thing that his filthy heart pumps round his body driving him on, making him think and believe that killing us is the answer to every problem he'll ever have.

He must realise that this is futile. That by killing and turning everyone he is eradicating his own food source which only serves to give him a finite existence.

'Church or pier Mr Howie?' Lani asks, breaking into my morbid thoughts.

'Church Lani.'

'Please say that's downhill,' Nick groans.

'Left and uphill again but only for a minute or two,' Lani turns and gives the struggling lad a huge gorgeous smile and I know it's just what he needs and must be making him feel like he's floating on air.

'DIG IN,' Clarence roars as we surge into yet another junction and turn to start working up the incline again. Growls come from Blowers as he lets some rage into his system, Tom looks tougher already and I can see Steven is struggling but determined. Nick worries me though, I can see he is really struggling to keep up with the relentless pace.

'Give me your axe,' I drop back and hold my arm out.

'I'm okay Mr Howie,' he pants.

'Now Nick,' I insist, a harder tone to my voice and he hands it over without question. Dave drops behind him and starts tugging his rucksack off, telling him to drop his arms down.

'I'm okay,' Nick protests again but is not left with any choice as Dave pulls the bag off and carries it one handed. Clarence drops back too, raises his water bottle over Nick's head upends it and pours the cool liquid over his face.

'Keep going Nick, you're doing well,' For once Dave doesn't rely on fear but adopts a softer tone urging him on.

'Go right,' Lani yells as we gain the next junction and I could kiss her for staggering the run like this instead of just assuming we could keep up with her and run straight up this hill. Cookey starts to flag next, he reaches the junction and starts well on the flat level ground but it's not long before I see his face grow pale with exhaustion and his steps begin to falter. Clarence notices too and drops back to grab his wrist and pull him on, yelling for someone to give him some water.

'They're gaining,' Dave keeps his voice calm but alerts us once more to the horde behind.

'We can stay flat for a while now,' Lani keeps us going along one wide avenue until we reach a crossroads. The hotel we used the night before is just down to the left with the seafront further down the hill providing a dazzling blue backdrop to the huge fire still raging away. We go over the crossroads and into the main town area, running past deserted shops and seeing more carnage from the night before. Decaying bodies and dried blood stains are everywhere. Dave runs to Lani and hands her Nick's bag then sprints off ahead disappearing into a shop doorway. Loud smashing sounds follow and within a few seconds he sprints back out carrying armfuls of Lucozade sports drinks. He runs back and hands them round to ragged thanks and grunts of approval. The flat Isotonic drink pumps welcome glucose into our systems, the risk of cramp is high but we need an instant energy fix more than anything or we'll grind to a halt. Tom, Steven and Lani aren't suffering the same as the rest of us, but then we've been solidly at it for the full nine days so far. Bad rest periods, sporadic food and constant movement has worn us down.

The drinks work, revitalising us within seconds and giving us just that extra bit of energy to keep our legs moving one foot in front of the other. That and the flat ground helps us push on. My legs feel like rubber, weak and shaky. My chest is heaving and I can feel a dull ache in the back of my head. The drink is downed within seconds and I can taste the syrup on my tongue and lips. Dave sprints off ahead again and this time he powers into the main doors of a large bar which already looks wrecked and destroyed with all the windows smashed and bits of furniture strewn about. He's gone longer this time and comes out just as we draw even with the building. Instead of carrying refreshing drinks he's got armfuls of spirit bottles, each one with the top unscrewed and a torn piece of rag hanging from the neck. He drops down and uses a lighter to ignite the rags.

'KEEP GOING,' He yells as we stop to help, his powerful voice repels us away and we do as we're told, jogging on as he picks the first bottle up and sends it high into the air. Two more are thrown before the first one impacts with a shattering whoosh and I glance back to see the liquid igniting into a thick pool of flame. Dave spot throws the bottles and creates a line of fire across the road before jogging back to us and taking Nick's bag from Lani.

'Good thinking mate,' I pant the words out between breaths, vowing to never smoke another cigarette again. The flames won't slow them but it will hurt a few and maybe ignite some clothes in their densely packed ranks. Through the town centre and we jog round to the left and up through the High Street. Again it starts off as a gentle incline but rapidly gets steeper until we're at risk of failing. But each time that happens we reach another junction and turn onto level ground.

'How....far?' Nick gasps.

'Just round the corner I promise Nick,' Lani urges him on and Clarence drops back to grasp his wrist again. 'There's the top there,' Lani points over the tops of the building ahead of us and sure enough we can see the top of a church tower pointing into the heavens. The sight does more than any sugary drink will ever do; it gives us hope and a visible finishing line.

'Dave, Lani, we need to make sure we can go straight in,' I shout out.

'Let me take Nick's bag,' Tom holds his hand out as Dave passes it over and I can see the young policeman still has energy left in his system. Lani passes me Nick's axe and they race off side by side. The young Thai woman easily keeping pace with the ex-special forces soldier.

'Fucking look at them two…' Cookey gasps. We urge, cajole, threaten and push each other on. Not one of us could have done this run on our own. The mental anguish would have been too great but together we've just about achieved it. Behind us the horde gain with every junction we pass. The church is dead ahead of us now. A massive structure just as Lani described with high narrow stained glass windows and a huge single tower that gradually thins to a sharp point at the very pinnacle.

'Lads,' I take a deep breath and judge that we've only got a couple of hundred metres left to go, 'we need to sprint…NOW….MOVE…NOW…' Clarence takes the order up and repeats it in his loud deep voice. With nothing left but pure spit we lengthen our strides and sprint it out. For the first few seconds it actually feels nicer to be moving at a different pace and the longer strides seem to stretch out sore thigh and calf muscles but that's it. Those few seconds. After that it's utter hell and quite possibly one of the hardest things I have ever done in my life.

But, we do it. We reach the church and the low wall running round it. Dave is off to the left waving us to follow him. We turn and head in his direction and he leads us down a side path to a surprisingly well built annexe. I was expecting a cheap structure cobbled together from the hard pressed church funds but this has been made with decent stone and strong modern windows. We go round to the back and into an open rear door. I have no idea who or how they got this open and I don't have the breath to ask right now. One by one we run inside and Dave slams the door shut then starts gathering furniture to stack against the inside of it. Creating a barricade behind us.

Rage fuels us and with grunts of animal anger we grab bookcases, desks, chairs and anything else we can find and ram them high and deep against the wall.

'Shutters,' Lani says and I glance round to see the inside of the windows have wooden shutters. They are more decorative than anything but they'll slow the horde down and we spin round the large room closing them to and snapping the thin locks down. A door opens into an office, through which is a thicker door leading to the church. Dripping sweat and swearing like the soldiers they are, Cookey and Blowers ransack the room in seconds until one of them is holding a big old-looking key up and shouting in triumph.

The key fits the door and it swings outwards, giving us the blessing we need as it means they won't be able to smash it in so quickly. The door is solid and would once have been the churches main rear door. We go through into the cool dark interior, our breathing and heavy footsteps echoing round the high room.

Dave gets the door closed, uses the key to lock it and slams thick bolts home at the top and bottom. We start towards the back looking for the main doorway that Lani mentioned but Dave waves us down, telling us to get our breath while Lani shows him the door which is further back along the church and off to one side.

'Two thick wooden doors, they'll hold for a while,' Dave calls out. I nod back from my position of bent almost double, my chest still heaving. The sweat pours off my forehead, big drops continually falling to a puddle at my feet.

'Water,' I shrug my bag down and take a bottle out, nodding and motioning for the others to do the same. They need little prompting and we gulp the liquid down quickly. Second bottles are opened then drained just as swiftly. Dave passes us on his inspection tour en route to the front where the vicar or priest or head god man would normally stand. He opens another door and slips out of view, returning a minute later.

'The tower entrance is through here, there's a toilet with running water too,' he calls across.

'Lads, get the bottles re-filled we could be here a while,' they scoop down to pick their bags up and head through the door. Muffled bangs suddenly sound out from the annexe then after a couple of minutes we hear more bangs on the main doors and the noise of glass windows being smashed. Looking up I see the windows of the church are not as narrow as I hoped but they are high up, depicting glorious images of saints bathed in golden light, crosses casting vibrant shadows and one that appears to show God bearing down on a demon like creature.

'Very apt,' I mutter and note that the window panes are lead lined. They'll take some damage to beat them out and make a hole big enough for a man.

'Good choice,' I shout to Lani as she appears from the door leading to the tower. She's used the running water to soak her hair and face and I watch as she steps through, pulling her wet shining hair back into a ponytail. The front of her top is drenched and clings to her frame. I glance away quickly hoping and praying she didn't notice me looking at her in that way.

'Thanks Mr Howie,' she replies and walks over to stand next to me, 'glad you let me come along then?'

'Very,' I smile at her and quickly look away again as she stares back holding eye contact.

'I'm er…I'll go and get some more water,' l can't believe that after running like that and everything that's happened I still get nervous around pretty girls, especially when they're wearing soaking wet tops and sexily pulling their hair back like that. Going through the door I see yet another solid wooden door propped open and thick stone steps leading away into the gloom. That must be the tower. A single bolt is on the inside but it will be enough to slow them down and we can do a fighting retreat. Buying time, that's all this is.
In the toilet I see the lads have stripped their tops off and are noisily splashing water over their bodies and holding their steaming heads under the running water, giving appreciative groans of pleasure. They make way as Dave and I enter and like them we strip, dunk our heads under and gasp as the beautifully cold water hits the backs of our necks. I soak my top in the running water and use it to wash the sweat away from my upper body. Clarence stands at the end wash basin bent over and keeps his huge bald head under the running water for long minutes.
I gulp the water down and keep going until I feel full knowing I'll be pissing every few minutes for the rest of the night. As I lift my head I catch my reflection for the first time in what feels like years. I'm not me anymore. Some bloke with a dark beard and curly dark hair stares back from the mirror.

He looks tanned and any trace of fat he once had on his face is gone.

I find a dry top in my bag and quickly pull it down over my head and tuck it into my trousers, remembering Dave doing this very same thing back in the supermarket when we met. Was it really only nine days ago?

'Ready?' the lads nod back, looking fresher and revitalised. We head back out into the main church room and hear loud bangs coming from all around us. Echoing off the big empty room. Groans sound out every few seconds and I look up at the darkening windows knowing that night can't be that far away.

We walk up towards the back of the church and peer into the recessed doorway. Two thick wooden doors are locked and bolted shut.

'It's too wide; if they break through together we won't be able to hold them. Grab some of these pews and shove 'em in there.' Easier said than done Howie. The long pew benches weigh a ton and it takes three of us per pew to manhandle it into the doorway. Apart from Clarence who drags one along on his own, scoring deep scratches into the ground from the end left on the floor.

'Get some more and turn them round to make them like hurdles. It'll slow them down and give us a chance to get a few shots in before we get through that door to the tower.' Again we pull more pews over and stagger them in lines going away from the door and leaving just enough room to squeeze through.

'Right, Blowers and Tom you stay close to that back door, Cookey, Nick and Steven you stay close to this door and try to rest. Get your shotguns ready and make sure you have cartridges to hand so you can re-load quickly,' the last bit is said more for the benefit of Tom, Steven and Lani but I know the others will keep a close eye on them.

'Fuck me Dave, that was evil,' I mutter as the lads start to sort through their bags and get their weapons ready.

'What was?'

'That bloody run! What did you think I meant?'

'Oh that, yeah it was quite long.'

'Quite long he says...'

'You did well though Mr Howie.'

'Thanks mate, the lads did well and that Lani is bloody fit.' He looks at me with that gleam in his eye that I've come to know so well.

'I meant fit as in running and stuff...'

'Yes Mr Howie.'

'Dave, I didn't mean it like I thought she's fit like hot or something.'

'Okay Mr Howie...is she not pretty then?'

'Fuck me Dave, are you asking my opinion on a woman?' I reply shocked.

'No Mr Howie.'

'You just did.'

'I was asking your view Mr Howie.'

'That's the same thing Dave.'
'Is it? Oh okay Mr Howie.'
'Well I guess we just wait now. I might have a cigarette…don't look at me like that Dave…'

Chapter Fourteen

'Why didn't you make them go faster?' Marcy demands as I stare up at the church looming above us and watch my babies probing the outside and looking for weaknesses.
'Because they still need air and blood the same as them…' I point to the church, 'and the same as you and I. Just because they're zombies doesn't make them fucking Olympic athletes Marcy.'
'Don't swear at me Darren.'
'I wasn't swearing at you my love I was swearing in conversation.'
'So that's Howie with the beard and the dark hair?'
'Yeah why? Fuck me Marcy you're always talking about him.'
'No I'm not Darren I was just asking. The small one was Dave, the big one Clarence who were the rest then? And who was that woman?'
'Three of them were Blowers, Cookey and Nick. They're the ones that shouted at us and said you were fit,' she gives a big grin at that, just like she did when she heard them shouting for me to send her over first back in that lane, 'I don't know who the others are.'
'That girl was pretty,' she muses.
'She was,' I reply and catch a sharp look from her, 'what? You were grinning when they said you looked fit.'
'That's different Darren.'

'How?'
'Because I'm still a woman and any woman likes to be complimented.'
'Yeah well…double standards if you ask me.'
'It's a good job I'm not asking you then isn't it,' she smiles acidly, 'so what now?'
'Wait for night, they'll get all powered up when it gets dark and we can start sending them in.'
'Right we need a plan, there are two ways in; one through those big doors and the other through that side building. I suggest we split them up and send one group in through the back, another attacking the main doors and some more smashing those big windows to see if we can get through there.' She stands with her hands on her hips looking like a sultry army general ordering troops into battle.
'What do you think?' She turns to face me.
'Well…'
'And once we've got an entry opened up we go back to the original plan and send the group one in first and then the rest as we discussed,' she cuts me off having clearly made her mind up.
'Did you hear what they said about my jeans,' I remember the insults and it's only now that we've had the time and the breath to mention it. 'I told you I looked stupid.'
'They're just jealous, what about the plan?'
'I felt stupid,' I mutter.

'Oh baby, don't look like that. They were just being mean for the sake of it. You look really nice dressed like that.'
'Do you think so?'
'Of course my baby Darren sweetie! Those nasty boys were just trying to upset you... come here and have a bite of my neck and feel all better,' she rubs my back as I nuzzle away and draw some refreshing blood down, 'there…that's better isn't it,' she says soothingly. I nod back and she wipes the blood from the corner of my mouth. 'Don't worry, you will have the last laugh when we get in there and eat them.'
'Okay baby,' I reply feeling better but still feeling stupid dressed in these stupid clothes.
'Now about the plan my sweetie, what do you think?' She smiles up at me and holds my hands in hers.
'It's a good plan baby.'
'Really?' She smiles, 'do you think so?'
'I think it's a great plan Marcy,' I nod and she grins proudly before turning back to watch the church. 'Okay my lover, can you split them up for me and send them where we said.'
'Okay baby,' she gives a little clap of joy as the horde suddenly stop moving freely and start responding to the control given from my mind. One group start towards the big doors. Another start towards the annexe and the last lot I get

mooching round for rocks, stones and anything that can be thrown to start breaking the windows. 'Oh we're so clever,' she claps excitedly again at the sight of our babies working to the plan she devised, 'You and I Darren my baby are destined for big things,' she throws her arms around me and slathers me in kisses before dropping her head down to bite into my neck and give herself some nourishment.
Tonight Howie. Tonight will be your last night on this earth so make the most of it you fucking little prick.

Chapter Fifteen

Daylight fades and the interior of the church grows gloomier and darker by the second. Stacks of candles are discovered in a big box at the back the church and these get handed round with strict instruction to make sure they don't fall over and set fire to anything, seeing as we're now effectively trapped.

'Also, if we start retreating then snuff 'em out as you fall back,' I call out and get a series of responses. With the candles lit the inside becomes soft and inviting. The stained glass windows reflect the flicker of the naked flames casting a warm orangey glow over everything. The general noise from outside suddenly ceases and the silence that follows becomes oppressive. All of us are waiting to see what happens next. What does happen is that the horde become directed and concentrated with two distinct attacks taking place. One at the main set of doors and, judging from the muffled sounds in that direction, the other from the annexe

'He's split them into teams,' Clarence says quietly looking first at the annexe door we came through then back to the main doors. Cooled off and re-hydrated we're left feeling a bit shaky and very drained from the massive expenditure of energy and excitement. Our breathing has become steadier and I can feel a sense of weariness starting to descend. Cigarettes are lit and I wonder when anyone was last allowed to smoke in here.

'How long will it take for them to get in?' Lani asks standing close to me and holding her shotgun one handed down at her side.

'Not long, it'll be night any minute and they'll get frenzied.'

'Once they get through we fall back to the tower and try to hold them off?'

'Yep, we'll get as many as we can. Try and reduce the numbers but ultimately it's about keeping them focussed and busy, letting Darren think he's got a chance of getting us otherwise there's a risk he'll move off to try and target our group.'

'Why isn't he doing that now? He could split his zombies and have some here and some going for the others, or just go for the others and leave us here.'

'I don't think he'll be able to control them so well if he splits them like that, also he knows that if he moves away from here we'll go after him and pick his horde off as they fall back, we are the primary objective I'm afraid.'

'But why? Why go after you so much? I get that there's history and stuff but if he left you alone you'd go back to your fort and he could do what he wants.'

'I don't know…he must be obsessed.'

'He knows we'll come after him,' Dave adds in a quiet voice, 'and kill every one of those things in the process.'

'Really? Would you do that if you had the choice to just live safely?'

'Yes we would because we wouldn't be living safely. It would only be a matter of time before he comes back and tries again. We've got no idea how long those things can last for, shit it could be years if they get enough nutrition to keep them going,' I reply.

'Or just a couple of weeks,' she says hopefully, 'if they're dead and their bodies are slowly dying then it can only be a matter of time. They don't eat and even if they could eat humans it wouldn't be enough to keep them going surely. Some of them look like they're falling apart.'

'That reminds me, Dave did you see the state of the zombies at the front of the horde?'

'I did Mr Howie. I think he's putting the worse ones at the front and keeping the others back.'

'He's doing what?' Nick calls across.

'You must have seen the state of those zombies at the front, they were falling apart. It looks like Darren is keeping the best ones for last.'

'What an utter cunt...sorry Lani,' Cookey spits.

'I've heard worse,' she replies.

'Oh here we go. Make ready,' I call out as all noise from outside ends. We all know what's about to happen but knowing it doesn't make it any less scary. And standing in an old church with hundreds of those things outside just increases the tension. Long seconds go by with nothing, no noise, no sounds apart from our breathing and thumping hearts. The hairs on the back of my neck stand up and then it hits.

Hundreds of voices bursting out as one. Howling into the night sky. Filling the air with horrendous screaming roars that send a shiver down my spine. The sound isn't human and it stands as testament to the sheer threat of what we're facing. Hundreds and hundreds of guttural voices going as loud as they can. High pitched, low pitched and every pitch in between but they're combined and synchronised and truly, utterly terrifying. Lani steps closer to me but she looks as poker faced as Dave. All of us stare round at the walls and I feel my skin crawling as the howls continue.

'KUM BA YAH MY LORD....KUM BY YAH!' Cookey bursts into song at the top of his voice making us all splutter with laughter, 'we're in a church,' he shrugs and starts again with Blowers and Nick joining in with him. By half way through the first verse we're all singing and screaming the words out as loud as possible, Clarence and Dave booming away with their deep bass voices. Giggles keep interrupting us but the sound fills the church.

'DARRENS A TWAT MY LORD KUM BA YAH' Cookey sings the first words as Blowers starts laughing hard. Again we join in with his new lyrics and blast the words out. The howling outside ceases and we all pause waiting for the frantic attack to begin but instead they start again, louder, harder and distinctly more aggressive. As soon as they start we start and the next few minutes are spent pitching our voices against each other with Cookey making up new versions for each verse. Then it's over and the nights work begins in earnest. Strong concerted attacks start at the main doors and from the annexe. Growls sound out and even from in here we can tell they're faster and moving with stronger purpose now. The first of the loud ragged thumps at the door cease and then start again with a combined fury echoing throughout the high walls.

'Form up,' I shout the order and we gather at the main doors, knowing it won't take long for them to break them open. The pews we stuffed in will slow them down but not for long.

'Fire in groups. Blowers you take Tom and Lani, Dave will take Cookey and Steven, Clarence you're with me and Nick. Keep an eye on that back door. We fall back steadily using the pews to fire from as we go. Unless they all come flying in at once in which case just run.'

'COVER,' Dave shouts at the same second as the windows all along the wall we're facing implode beneath the force of launched missiles. Glass fragments fly deep into the room as rocks bounce down on the wooden pews. We scoot forward and press ourselves against the wall either side of the main door. With no windows directly above us we should be fairly safe. Rocks, stones, and smashed up paving slabs come flying through the windows. More glass shatters and I wince at the damage being caused to such a lovely old building. A cacophony of noise clamours all around us. Howling from the undead screaming in hunger and frustration, loud solid bangs from the doors, the splintering crash of breaking glass. We stay quiet, with Dave and me peering round the edges of the recess checking the doors.

'Doors breaching,' Dave says loud enough for everyone to hear. The doors slowly start to give under the merciless weight of bodies being slammed against them again and again.

My rate of breathing increases and my heart slams inside my chest. Sharp focus comes into my eyes. A sense of excitement. Adrenalin getting ready to be released. Rage and fury start to build but I won't let them control me now. The cost was too high and I faltered the last time. It needs to be focussed and used sparingly. Kill quickly. Move quickly. Conserve energy. The doors start to give, gradually splintering and creaking with each successive thump. Then they split as the locks give and a small gap forms in the middle.

'Ready Dave?' I shout over to my friend. We lock eyes smiling at each other and seeing the sheer impatience for it to begin.

'Yes Mr Howie,' he growls back.
'Blowers, make ready to fire...wait...wait...NOW!' The doors give, slamming back against the pews and giving enough gap to allow the first two snarling monsters through. Blowers, Tom and Lani lurch round to face into the recessed area and unload six shots within a split second massacring the first two zombies.
'HOLD!' I raise my hand and watch as the next lot negotiate the bodies of the first two blocking the path. The bodies get pulled back and I realise Darren must be close enough to watch and control them. Instead of powering through they focus on slamming into the doors again and again, trying to force the gap to widen.
'Dave, Cookey, Steven go up and fire through the gap...NOW' they surge in with Dave going low to fire his barrels out through the gap, Steven fires above him and Cookey jumps in as Steven drops back. A very slight pause and they start again, harder and more powerful. I catch a glimpse through the gap of one of the bodies being used as a battering ram. Held by several others it is slammed repeatedly into the gap pulping the already destroyed body.
'My lot....NOW,' I drop down, copying Dave's movement so I can fire with Clarence above me. Our shots are taken and we drop back. Another pause and then a huge crash as Darren sends a whole group surging forward to slam into the

doors. The impact sends the pews back a couple of inches and before we have time to react and push them back another round crashes in and forces the gap to widen even more.

'FALL BACK,' we move out and take cover behind the first of the pews. More crashes and the doors widen with each massive impact. Then four of them burst through, snarling and scrabbling to be the first ones to take our flesh.

'FIRE,' Blowers shouts and his group stand to unload all their shots then drop down to quickly re-load. The four undead become dead again as hundreds of pellets rip them to pieces but more take their place.

'FIRE,' Dave's turn to shout and they fire into the recessed area, shredding the zombies to pieces. As quick as they fall more surge in and I shout my turn. Firing our weapons and dropping down to re-load as Blowers takes over. Blowers, Dave, Me and we repeat the action again and again until the bodies start to pile up and create a natural obstacle.

Loud bangs sound from the door behind us but its outward opening and will take more to break through.

'Windows,' Dave yells. I look up to see an undead clinging onto the windowsill and trying to rip the lead lining out. He grasps the lining between his hands while more zombies underneath yank him down hard, bringing the lead with him.

'Fuck me that's clever,' Cookey shouts as we reload. More undead appear at the windows, hoisted up high and ripping the lead down forming holes big enough to get bodies through.
'I'll take them,' Dave shouts as more zombies appear at the windows. We continue to fire into the killing ground of the doorway. The reduced range of the shotguns is vastly outweighed by the awesome fire power and the slaughtered corpses stack up. Blood and gunky pieces of flesh coat the walls, dripping down to pool on the floor. The doors and pews get peppered again and again by the pellets and the room reeks from the constant firing. Eardrums hurt and heads ache but they go unnoticed as we fire again and again.
A single howling zombie balances on the narrow sill above our heads and drops down. Dave is there instantly knives drawn and the thing is dispatched within a second, its head dropping from its neck and rolling across the flagstone floor. The back door is taking a hammering but holding firm. More undead clamber onto the windowsills and start dropping in only to be met by Dave spinning and dancing through them with his deadly knives. Not one of them takes more than a couple of steps before they're made dead again. Steven, Tom and Lani all stand with their mouths open watching mesmerised as Dave dances with his athletic grace, stretching, kneeling, leaping and spinning.

'Wait till he gets warmed up,' Clarence shouts above the noise.

'Start moving back,' I yell out in alarm as the fresh surge of zombies coming through the doors pick up some of the corpses and start using them as shields, gaining ground as the pellets slam into the cadavers but lack the power to rip all the way through the meat.

As one we move back a couple of pews, Blowers taking the time to extinguish the candles as we retreat. Lani drops her shotgun for a second and runs at the undead falling through the windows with her meat cleaver drawn and ready. She slams the blade into a neck and extends her foot to kick it back before spinning round to slice the blade deep across a zombie face.

'Keep firing,' I shout and we let rip with the shotguns. All order is gone and we all fire at will, re-loading and firing both our barrels into the mass. The cadavers being used as shields quickly get shredded and discarded but fresh ones are swiftly taken up.

'Time to go, FALL BACK,' I yell out as they almost reach the edge of the threshold. Once there they'll be able to spill out to both sides and start surrounding us. We fall back steadily, kicking candles out with our feet and plunging the room further into darkness. Dave drops back towards our group and kills the zombies coming at him rather than rushing into their ranks and leaving us exposed.

'REAR DOOR,' Blowers shouts as the wood splinters from the sustained battering.

'ON IT,' Clarence bellows and shoves his shotgun into his backpack, taking up his axe he marches to the door and stands ready to repel.

'KEEP GOING,' I shout and we fire our weapons at them as we negotiate the pews. They breach the edge of the recess and surge into the church, moving off to the sides. The shotguns are now rendered useless as they fan out. Mine gets shoved back into my bag and like Clarence I take up my axe and grip it two handed. Ready. Waiting. Eyes fixed. Growls sound out from zombies and humans as we retract into a tight bunch and edge back closer and closer to the door.

They attack. Suddenly and with ferocious intent and it's down to this again. Hand weapons and fighting to survive. My axe comes alive in my hands. An old friend that feels familiar and just right. I swing out slicing deep into a neck and severing the head. Pull back and strike out again cleaving a skull open and spilling brains onto the floor. A quick glance shows me the annexe door is breached and Clarence is putting his own axe to deadly use, repeatedly chopping into each zombie that tries to clamber through the broken door. He checks round and sees us retreating and drops back to join the group.

As we reach the door, Dave, Clarence and I take the front and fight them back while the others drop through one by one.

I go next leaving the two best fighters repelling the attacking zombies. Clarence next and Dave stands his ground as we draw breath and watch in wonder as the man holds steady and kills anything that dares get close to him.

'CLARENCE…PULL ME QUICK AND SLAM THE DOOR,' Dave's voice booms out. He knows that to take a step backwards will send them surging into the doorway and we'll never be able to close it. With on hand on the open door Clarence leans out and grabs the back of Dave's rucksack. With a mighty heave he pulls Dave clean off his feet and into the room with us. Slamming the door shut with his other hand he drops Dave and shoves his body against the door. A single key lock holds the door but it's enough to hold for a second while we cross into the tower stairwell and slam that door behind us too. Again just a single bolt gets rammed home.

'Get re-loaded and have water if you need it,' with the door closed I speak into pitch black until Dave and Nick rummage through their bags and turn small torches on giving us enough light to see.

'Is there another door at the top?' I ask Dave.

'No, the stairs spiral up to a landing then start again. They get much narrower as they go higher.'

'Okay, original plan then. We retreat slowly and keep cutting them down as we go. Everyone okay? Anyone hurt?'

'My feelings are a bit hurt Mr Howie...I think I might need some counselling,' Cookey jokes.

'You need sectioning mate,' Blowers adds, 'fucking Kum by Yah? Where did that come from?'

'That was brilliant,' Tom laughs, 'I remember singing that at school.'

'See, stick with us Tom it's a laugh a minute...just don't let yourself get caught alone with Blowers,' Cookey says in a serious tone.

'Eyes front,' Dave interrupts to the sound of the first door splintering open followed a second later by loud thumps at the door just a few feet below us.

'Get into pairs, how are we for cartridges?'

'We're okay but they won't last long if we keep that rate of fire up.' Dave answers.

'Stick with the shotguns for now and we'll switch to hand weapons when we get further up...here they come.' The doors bursts open and the space instantly fills with the snarling faces of the undead.

'Change of plan,' I shout and step forward with my axe, swinging it down to chop deep into the shoulder of the first one through the door. 'Use hand weapons now and save the shotguns for when they send the best ones through...Tom up front with me.' The staircase is wide enough for us to stand side by side and have enough room to swing down and batter them away. Tom responds quickly, joining me at the front as they pour through the door and start climbing the stairs. Dave drops down behind us and holds his torch so it shines down the stairs illuminating them and trying to blind them at the same time.

Undead rush forward and I slice them down, cutting heads off and very slowly giving ground. They quickly muster and start attacking in greater numbers. Snarling vicious beasts with clawed hands, bared teeth and a wild feral way of moving. Tom does well for his first proper fight and he soon gets the hang of it, slashing away and cutting down into their heads. The bodies drop and roll backwards but soon get trampled underneath the ever encroaching fetid zombies.

'Next two,' I yell out, keen to swap round and conserve our energy and knowing how tired my arms got when I first started swinging my axe about so knowing Tom must be feeling it.

'Ready Mr Howie,' Cookey right in my ear. I press back against the wall as the lad steps past me and starts cutting them down. Breathing hard I move further up the stairs as Nick takes over from Tom.

'You did well mate,' I say to Tom between breaths.

'Thanks,' Tom looks at me with a glint in his eye that I've seen many times from the lads after a fight and I know he'll do well from now on.

The horde presses the attack and with every minute that passes it feels their attack becomes fiercer, more ferocious and determined. Slowly giving ground, one step at a time it's not long before Cookey and Nick swap round with Blowers and Steven and I realise our two best combatants are holding their turn for when they're really needed the most. Blowers, a proven warrior steps in to take his turn, swinging out and culling their numbers with now practised ease. Steven seems wild though, he swings out too hard and repeatedly slams the axe into the wall at his side jarring his arms and damaging the blade. His screams of fury seem more fear than anger. It's too dark to see his face but I already know there'll be a wild look on it. He seems too intent, too angered and far too eager as he hacks and swings away with wild abandon. Both Dave and I shuffle closer getting ready to take action. Clarence steps down and taps my shoulder, motioning that he'll take over from the skinny lad. 'Steven, move back,' he ignores me and keeps swinging out, missing more than he's hitting and I notice that his strikes are getting more arms and torso's than heads or necks. Blowers has to work harder to compensate for the ones Steven keeps missing and it's not long before they are pressing closer towards us.

'MR HOWIE!' Blowers yells in alarm at the sudden surge of bodies pushing forward. Dave is there instantly, shoving Blowers aside with his shoulder and dropping down a couple of steps to hold a central position. Holding the torch in his mouth his arms spin out, slashing the blades across throat after throat. Sprays of hot blood pump out as the bodies sink down to slide down the already wet slippery steps. He drops down and quickly moves the blade amongst their legs severing Achilles tendons and more bodies sink down. They use their arms to keep clawing and dragging themselves up but they create a moving obstacle that the others find difficult to negotiate. Steven, seeing the pause in fighting lunges in front of Dave and starts hacking away at the packed zombies. Screaming with fury he slips on the wet steps and crashes to the floor, sliding down the stairs until his body impacts on the front of the horde.

We roar in warning and surge down to beat them back but it's too late. Teeth are already sinking into Steven's legs and thighs. He screams with agony and tries beating them off with his hands. Clarence, Dave and I all work like demons to slash down, hack at them and drive them back. Clarence, roaring like a bear scoops up a man size zombie that writhes and gnashes in his hands. The giant man launches the snarling creature down into the front of the horde and the momentum sends them all staggering and falling away.

In the brief pause Dave drops and grabs Steven by the collar, dragging him away from the front as Clarence and Lani take front position, Lani taking up Steven's fallen axe instead of her meat cleaver. 'Fuck it,' I spit the words out as I see the ragged mess of Steven's legs. The material has been torn away, flesh is hanging in strips down to the bone. Blood pisses out everywhere and the poor lad is screaming in agony, begging to be saved and not left to die. Tom turns away too distraught at seeing his friend dying. I quickly draw my pistol from my belt and fire a single round into his skull blasting the back of his head off. Looking up I see Dave, Blowers and the rest staring at me before turning back to the matter in hand.

'Blowers, keep Tom at the back.'

'Got it.'

'I'm okay Mr Howie,' Tom shouts in the darkness but there isn't time to discuss it and I look down to see Clarence and Lani forced to give more ground, moving steadily back towards us.

As the stairwell turns into an ever decreasing circle so the steps become narrower until only one can stand out front battering them back. Likewise they can only send a few cramped zombies forward at once but they do send them. They keep sending them. They send more and more and we rotate our turns and swing our axes until our chests are heaving from the effort and our arms and shoulders are on fire and every few minutes we are forced to move back.

Some of the zombies take up the tactic they showed downstairs and use the dead cadavers as shields to hide behind while they charge up at us. Slowly at first then more and more of them try it until every zombie that comes up is somehow holding a dead body in front of it. The end result is the same but it takes far more effort and wastes vital energy hacking into corpses that are already dead and we give more ground until we're getting onto the first landing.

Someone hands me a bottle as I step back from my turn and I first pour the water over my sweat soaked skin before gulping it down quickly. No jokes from Cookey now. No banter or defiant shouting. This is messy, draining hard work and our low energy levels are dropping by the second. I realise I can see better and looking round I see a window set into the side of the wall with bright moonlight shining through.

'Get the shotguns ready,' I call out, 'someone break that window and see what it's like down the bottom.' Cookey uses the shaft of his axe to beat the glass out and I hope to hell it falls down and slices Darren's face off. He rakes the shaft round clearing the shards away and sticks his head out.

'How is it?' I shout over to him.

'You don't want to know,' he ducks back in, 'fucking loads of them down there.'

'Still?' Nick asks.

'We're only killing a few at a time,' Dave explains.

'Fuck...' Cookey says, 'fuck...' he repeats and like the rest of us he shrugs it off and stands up ready with his shotgun.

'Ready,' he shouts and strides over to the top of the stairs. We join him and shout for Clarence and Lani

to fall back. Lani goes first, ordered by Clarence. She scoots through and drops down with her chest heaving. I pick up a bottle of water and go to hand it to her but she's dropped down on her hands and knees breathing hard. She's fit enough to run for miles but swinging a heavy axe has clearly drained her.
'You're doing well,' I say quietly. The first of the shotguns fires, followed by more and the sounds of the guns breaking open and fresh cartridges being shoved in.
'Rest for a minute,' I twist the lid from the top of the water bottle and use one hand to lift her chin up while I pour water gently down her face and then the back of her neck. She breathes with her mouth open and even in this light I can see she looks flushed. She turns round to rest with her back against the wall and I hand her the bottle, 'drink and rest for a minute.'
'Thanks,' she says softly and presses the bottle to her lips. Standing up I see Blowers and Cookey looking down with concern.
'She okay?' Cookey asks.
'I'm fine,' she says her voice as strong as ever.
'Well get back down and fuck 'em up some more then,' Cookey retorts and gets a middle finger in response from Lani.
We rest for a minute or so, using the shotguns to blast them back down and when my turn comes I

watch with satisfaction as the power of the weapons stands true and blows their heads apart.

'They've stopped,' Nick shouts as he aims his unfired gun into the darkness. We gather round and stare down, looking at mangled bodies but nothing else.

'Get ready to move back,' I say quietly guessing Darren is gathering a load to send up together and press the attack.

'MR HOWIIIIEEEEEEE,' my guess is right as his mocking tones bounce up the stairs to me.

'Smithy, how are you mate?'

'Er...its Darren now please Mr Howie,' he yells back.

'Oh is it...'

'Yeah it is...how are you doing up there? We got one didn't we?'

'Just the one so far Smithy, not that good considering how many we've killed.'

'Oh I've got plenty more yet.'

'Have you now...tell you what Smithy, why don't you grow a pair and come up yourself? Me and you Smithy, no weapons, just me and you.'

'Yeah right! What and that little cuntrunt Dave is just going to stand and watch?'

'They won't do anything Smithy, you have my word. Come up and we'll end this.'

'Oh Mr Howie...'

'You're a fucking coward Smithy. You send all these things to do something you're too scared to do yourself.' I bellow down.
'FUCK YOU…' He screams in utter rage.
'NO DARREN…' a female voice yells
'Get off me Marcy; I'm not a fucking coward.'
'Yes he is…' Cookey shouts.
'Marcy? Is that your name? I saw you earlier. I'm Howie, it's very nice to meet you Marcy.' I keep my tone very polite knowing it'll wind him up.
'Hello Howie,' a sultry voice floats up and I look round to see Blowers and Cookey smiling, eyebrows raised.
'So you don't want to send Smithy up then?' I ask.
'No,' she answers simply.
'Well how about you then? It's not too late Marcy. You've picked the wrong side.'
'Thank you Howie but I'm fine where I am,' a hint of humour in her voice, 'er…I don't have to call you Mr Howie too do I?'
'Of course not, so how's this going to end Marcy? When will Smithy realise we won't stop until every one of those things is dead…including him.'
'Oh Darren won't lose Howie,' her sultry husky tones sound out, 'maybe you should come and join us…I would like that very much,' her voice drops to an even more sultry tone and I just catch the sound of muffled voices. Darren getting angry at her overtly flirtatious manner.

'Well….that's a very kind offer but I will have to pass.'
'That's a great shame Howie…we could have gotten to know each other better.'
'True, tell me, seeing as you can talk and think the same as before. Why stick with Darren? Come with us and maybe we can find a cure. We've got doctors and equipment that can help you.'
'Well now Howie…if I came up those stairs and *surrendered* myself to you, your lovely boys would kill me instantly.'
'No they won't Marcy. I promise you.'
'But how would you know I wouldn't *bite you* Howie…would you *tie me up*?' the tone she inflects is so downright flirty that my mouth drops open in surprise, looking round I can see most of the others are the same too, apart from Cookey who is grinning like a Cheshire cat and loving every minute of it.
'Come up here and try it you rancid diseased whore,' Lani's voice booms down the stairs to the shock of everyone else. 'And it is *Mr* Howie to you…bitch.'
'Oh Howie…got yourself a lady friend. Is that the girl with the dark hair I saw you with? She is very pretty…for an Asian girl that is.'
'You said we couldn't use racism.'
'Shut up Darren,' Marcy snaps back in a harsh tone.
'Yeah shut up Darren,' Cookey mocks, 'do as you're told there's a good boy.'

'Was that her idea to wear those trousers like that Smithy?' Nick shouts down.
'Fuck off Nick,' his voice screams up which sets the lads laughing.
'Yeah Nick...fuck off,' Cookey mocks again in a camp voice while I look at Lani in puzzlement. She glances round to see me staring and smiles, giving a faint shrug of her shoulders, 'Sorry but I didn't like her,' she says quietly.
'No, don't apologise...its fine.' Dave slips behind me and draws my pistol from my belt. Silently he starts creeping down the stairs with the handgun and torch held out in front of him. He looks round at Cookey and motions for him to keep going.
'Smithy...How many boy zombies have you bummed so far?'
'Fuck you Cookey... I'm not Blowers.'
'Ha, Blowers even the twat super zombie knows you like bumming,' Cookey laughs.
Dave reaches the bend and quickly darts round, switching the torch on and firing down with quick successive bangs. I hear the sound of bodies falling and more scrambling to move away. Dave finishes the magazine and climbs back up.
'Almost but he was covered,' Dave shakes his head as the horde suddenly start charging up with a nasty snarl.
Back to work we go. Using the shotguns to drive them back but quickly giving ground as they really press the attack home. Within seconds we're

across the landing and round the next bend at the start of the next flight of stairs. Each one of us works to re-load and fire as quickly as possible. We get constant kills in and with every gun firing twice I know we must be culling their numbers, little by little but at least we're doing it.
'Hand weapons,' I give the order to switch seeing the narrower stairwell on the second flight and knowing it'll be easier to hold them back. Taking first stand I ready myself as they pour across the landing and sweep round the curvature. Axe ready , I swing out chopping the first one down and lifting the double blade up and into the groin of the next one. They both tumble down and I slam down into the next one making it fall into the heap of the other two. The next one uses the heap of bodies as a spring board and launches itself at me. The axe catches him mid-air and slams him into the wall but I have to give ground in case they keep doing it. More kills and I swap round when my arms start to feel jaded. Taking it in turns we hack and kill, slowly reducing their numbers. The minutes tick into hours and we slowly rotate, giving ground slowly but surely. Drinking water and breathing hard every time we take a break. Lani insists on taking her turn again and stands out front with determination and sheer guts. Swinging the axe with all her might and chopping them down one after the other.

I hand her a bottle of water as she drops back to let Clarence take over and she gulps it down after giving me a quick smile. All of us, well maybe apart from Dave, feel the fatigue kicking in. Tiredness starts creeping into our limbs and any conversation we have is stilted and abrupt. Tom takes his turn quietly and fights with passion, clearly using the time to give vengeance for the loss of his close mate. Then it's back to me and I take my glorious axe and stand in position.
The first one comes charging in with a howl, drooling lips pulled back to show me his yellow stained teeth. As I slam the axe down into his head something snaps in me. The righteous glory of battle descends and I feel my limbs come back to life. Just as they did at the end of that big fight when I was on my knees. Each swing of the axe seems calculated and intense. Every slash takes one down and I'm already eyes up watching the next one come. The pressure builds in me and I roar my defiance out. Screaming into the darkness I kill them quickly. We've been giving ground since we started but maybe we should take a bit back. I step down and repeat my killing blows, watching undead after undead drop before my eyes. My eyes that paint the target for the axe. The axe that is as much a part of me as my heart. My heart that beats pure clean blood and sends me down to do battle with these filthy spawning creatures. Every step I take down is a victory for mankind. They keep

coming but my movements get faster and faster until I am one with my weapon. Slicing left, right, up, down. Each one a killing blow. My feet are firm and my steps do not falter and I take back the ground we gave to them.

Time ceases to flow. Everything is paused as I descend into the bowels of darkness. I don't need light to show me the way. I don't need anything but what I am right now. In this holy place I feel strong, powerful yet strangely humbled. Humbled that I have been allowed to use this gift in such a way. They come at me harder and faster than ever before. They surge and lunge. They gnash their teeth but I smile at them. I show them a death full of grace and pity but one delivered with brutal honesty. Still they come and still they die and still I keep moving forward. I hear nothing but the sound of the axe moving through the air. I see nothing but the target in front of me.

The landing. I move across the landing and tread firmly over the bodies already downed. The stairwell is wider here and I give thanks that I can stretch my swings out and move with more room. I plough on. Nothing exists. Time and space are a memory, a thing of inconsequential nothingness that doesn't belong in this place. Left. Right. Up. Down. I kill and they die.

Back at the top of the landing I feel a burst of strength and my movements become even faster and I clear them away with such speed that it all

seems too slow for me. Then suddenly there's a gap and I'm standing at the top of the landing staring out of the window at the bright moon.
'Drop back Mr Howie,' Dave pulls the axe from my hands and takes my place at the top of the stairs. I do as instructed and move back. Everyone stares at me, mouths hanging open and eyes wide. I feel tired now. Bone weary and tired but I feel peace within me and I take the bottle of water that Lani hands me and drink the cool satisfying liquid down.
'Thanks, that was nice,' I hand the bottle back and she stares at me with a puzzled expression. I look to my right and see Clarence watching me too, he is shaking his head and a small wry smile forms on his mouth.
'That's twice you've done that now boss,' he rumbles.
'Ah well, I fancied a change of tactic for a minute.'
'Fuck me Mr Howie…I hope I never piss you off,' Cookey says with a look of such awe that it makes me feel uncomfortable.
'Nick, have you got any smokes mate?'
'Yeah sure, hang on,' he drags a packet out from a pocket and taps one out, hands it to me with a lighter. Once lit I inhale and lean against the wall with my back to everyone else. The sense of peace is stunning. A tranquil soothing sensation that comes up from deep within me, but leaves me so tired and weary.

'Here, I was saving this but you can have it...I think you might need it,' Lani hands me a bottle of coke. I smile back and twist the cap off before taking a big gulp of the wonderfully sugary fluid.

'Ah that is bloody nice,' I hand it back, 'pass it round, I think we all need some.' There is a yell from Dave and suddenly we're moving back from a fresh attack pressed home by an incredibly fierce load of undead.

Driven back we slowly ascend the stairs as this new lot drive forward with an as yet unseen level of violence. These must be the best ones that Darren was holding back. They look less decayed than any other zombies I've seen. The only visibly injuries are just small bite marks to their necks.

'I think you've pissed them off,' Blowers yells as he fights like a demon himself. He slams his axe back and forth but we're driven further back and up the stairs.

We start using shotguns firing from underneath the person out front such is the desperation of their attack. Firing and re-loading and still giving ground. Higher and higher up the narrowing staircase we go, twisting round and round. Clarence takes over at the front but the restricted space makes it hard for him to move easily. He fights for a few minutes still being pressed back.

'We're at the top,' Lani shouts. Glancing round I see the moonlight shining down onto the stairs.

'Fall back and get ready to close the door,' I shout loudly and the others swiftly obey, running up into the clear air. Staying right behind Clarence, Dave and I guide him backwards until he suddenly flattens himself against the wall and Dave takes over, using his knives to good effect in the confined space. With short, sharp slashes he kills them one by one. Leaving Dave to hold the stairs I stagger out into what I was hoping would be lovely cool air but instead feels far too warm and muggy for the middle of the night.

Leaning over the chest high railing I look down and see a few bodies dotted about but not too many.

'Cookey, are there less than when you looked earlier?' He leans over and examines the grounds round the bottom.

'A lot less Mr Howie,' he grins that infectious grin and drops back down. The platform skirts the square shaped tower in a narrow walkway. There are no other exits so we have to hope and pray we can hold them off.

'Just a couple more hours and it'll be getting light,' Blowers stares out at the darkened town and the orange glow coming from the fire raging in the distance.

'If we get out of this I'm going straight down to the beach to cool off in the sea,' Nick sighs and wipes the sweat from his face.

'I'm up for that mate,' I reply.

'That's after the cooked breakfast with loads of toast and coffee,' he adds wistfully.
'And fresh orange juice,' I add to the dream and regret it instantly as it makes the reality taste as sour as it really is.
'Who is going after Dave?'
'Er…Mr Howie…' Tom says suddenly with a tone of urgency. I join him leaning over the rail and staring down at the ground. At the dark figures standing around something that flickers and flares brightly. Then more of them flare up until there's a row of bright things. My tired eyes take a few seconds to send the images to my brain for processing and what I'm looking at banishes all tiredness within a split second.
'Mr Howie they've pulled back again,' Dave yells through the door.
'I bet they have…they're gonna burn us out.' I shout back. With alarmed yelps everyone rushes over to look down. The flaming things, whatever they are get carried towards the church and out of view.
'They're setting the church on fire,' Clarence says, his voice calm and natural.
'Options? We can fight our way down or try and wait it out,' I race round the walkway peering over the side. The tower is high and it would mean instant death to jump from here. The tower is joined to the main building but that's still a good 15 feet below us and the roof is sharply angled. A wrong landing and we would just slide down the

side and fall into their laps. The only option is to go back down the stairs and fight our way through the horde and out into the open. Unless Darren has pulled all his zombies back and left us a clear exit which is not likely. Not likely at all.

'Here Mr Howie,' Nick calls out. He is shining his torch over the side, 'thick drainpipe,' he points, as I rush over to him.' That should hold our weight.'
The wrought iron drainage pipe is bolted to the wall and must be strong if it's to take all the water from this roof.

'It might hold Dave and Lani, maybe us but definitely not Clarence,' I reply.

'It might do Mr Howie, I'll try it,' Nick clambers up to the ledge and starts easing himself over the other side.

'What's he doing?' Clarence joins me looking down and I tell him about the drainpipe. We watch as Nick leans down and starts tugging on the pipe, then holding his weight with both hands he rests his foot on it and slowly shifts his weight.

'It's not moving,' he stares back up.

'Okay, get back up mate, Clarence can you pull that wiring down' I point up to the thick electric cable snaking round the tower and providing a power supply to the lamps positioned to illuminate the spire at night. With his bare hands Clarence yanks one end from the lamp and follows it round snapping it free from the wall connectors. The rest gather at the railings looking down at the drainpipe Nick points out.

'Dave are you okay?' I yell through the door.

'FINE,' Dave bellows back and I can see he's holding ground and not given an inch yet.

'They're setting the church on fire trying to burn us out.'

'ARE THEY? OKAY MR HOWIE.' Nothing fazes that man. I could have told him Darren had an atomic bomb he was detonating and the response would have been the same. Back outside I watch as Clarence ties one end of the cable to the railings and drops it down to rest by the drainpipe.

'I'll go first,' Lani says confidently, 'I'm the lightest by far so let me try it.' A whooshing sound reaches our ears and we crane over the side to see strong light now coming from the broken windows, illuminating the grassy area surrounding the church. Without another word Lani tightens the straps on her bag and wedges Steven's axe down the back of it before climbing over the railings. Grasping the electric cable she starts lowering herself down. Rapidly dropping hand under hand and lowering herself into the darkness. Nick shines the torch down and we watch as she runs out of cable before reaching the bottom and switches her hands onto the drainpipe for the last few feet before she drops nimbly onto the roof. Smiling she gives a thumbs up.

'Blowers, you go next and provide cover in case anything happens down there.'

'On it,' he copies Lani, shoves his axe down the back of his bag and climbs over the railings. With a grim smile and nod he takes the cable and starts lowering himself down, switching to the drainpipe as the cable runs out and dropping down onto the roof. Nick follows them, repeating the actions and straining with the effort of holding his weight on the thin cable. He takes longer to swap from cable to pipe but eventually with a thud he too drops down. Tom then Cookey go down easily enough until there's just me, Dave and Clarence left.

'Dave, we've found a way down. There's an electric cable and drainpipe running down the side of the tower onto the church roof. There's just me and Clarence to go, the rest are down already.'

'I'll hold them here Mr Howie, you go and I'll catch you up.'

'Dave, when Clarence shouts you start coming. Got it?'

'Got it.' He continues his killing spree which has slowed down remarkably from either him killing them all or because the fire is raging too much to send anymore up.

Outside I stuff my axe down into my bag and climb over. Taking the cable in my hands I copy what the others did and start lowering myself down. The cable bites into my fingers and hurts but it's just thick enough to grip and I use my feet to scrabble as I steadily get lower. The cable runs short as I'd seen with the others and I reach out to grasp the drainpipe which holds firmly and within a few seconds I'm standing on the roof with one foot either side of the apex.

'Feel the roof Mr Howie,' Cookey urges me. I drop my palm down and feel the warmth radiating through the rough tiles and the strong smell of wood smoke reaches my nose. Glancing over I can see plumes of smoke starting to waft from the empty windows. Clarence's huge bulk straddles the railings and he starts dropping down much faster than the rest of us did. He's either very experienced at doing this or he's shitting himself that his heavy weight will snap the cable. At the same point as us he reaches over and shifts his weight from cable to pipe and continues his downward journey. A popping noise sounds out and a bolt falls to land between my feet, rolling off down the side of the roof. More follow as the drainpipe creaks under the heavy burden of Clarence. With a few metres still left to go it breaks free from the wall and swings down with Clarence still attached. He manages to get his feet underneath him, ready to try and land properly but the force of his weight sends him straight through the tiles. The others burst away desperately trying to avoid being crushed. Scorching heat rushes from the hole in the tiles and I crab forward to see Clarence clinging onto the drainpipe edged over the hole he made, his feet dangling above the raging inferno below him.

'Hold the ends of the pipe,' Shouting out I grasp one end and watch as the others snake over to stop it sliding off. Clarence does one mighty pull up and starts levering himself up, grabbing the sides of the roof and not risking his weight on the pipe any more than he has too. We grab at his arms and backpack, pulling his enormous weight out from the hole. The heat is intense and I can feel my face sweating already. The drainpipe starts to shift and slide as the edges of the hole crumble and give way. We dig in and with shouts of pure effort we inch him out bit by bit. The hole gets larger as Clarence strains and wrestles to get his upper body out enough to swing his legs up. Gradually he gets out and lies panting for a few seconds.

'Are you hurt?' I start to check his legs for burns but other than feeling hot there doesn't seem to be any damage.

'I'm okay,' he rumbles back, 'did Dave get down?' On hearing his words we all look up to see Dave dangling from the cable with one hand and patiently waiting for us to stop pissing about. Clarence springs to his feet and grabs the drainpipe, clenching it between his muscled arms he leans it against the wall just to the side of Dave. Blowers and Nick brace Clarence as Dave nimbly swings out and starts a quick descent down the pipe, placing one foot on Clarence's bald head he slides down his back to land with a wry grin.

'Sorry about your head Clarence,' he says flatly as ever.

'No you're bloody not,' Clarence rubs his smooth head grumbling away to himself.

'Time we weren't here,' I mutter quietly and start walking along the apex one foot either side and heading for the far end.

'They've seen us,' Dave bellows, well if they hadn't they would have bloody heard us that's for sure. 'I'll go first,' Dave adds.

'Piss off, you're not having all the fun,' I reach the end and look down. Too high to jump but I spot a grassy bank a couple of feet out from the end. Turning round I plant my arse on the tiles and draw my axe from behind me. Letting myself slide down the now very hot tiles I reach the lowest point and jump down to land heavily on the top of the grass bank. The axe falls from my grasp as I land and I don't have time to go for it before the first of the undead lunge at me. Fortunately only a couple have made it round this end so far. I charge at him and slam my forehead into the middle of his face. Pain explodes behind my eyes but it does the trick and we both go down with me landing on top of him. My fists reign down smashing the shit out of his head before I jump back and draw the pistol from my belt. He's up instantly and I fire several times into his face then lift the pistol and fire at the next one coming. He drops but more are behind him and coming fast. Dave drops to my side and instantly draws his knives.

'Get your axe,' and he's off charging them with a deep roar. Changing magazines I re-holster the weapon and scoop my axe up before racing forward and joining my friend. We stand together hacking them down as more of our group slide down the roof and land heavily on the top of the bank, sprawling out with yelps of pain. A shotgun blasts out to my side and I see Blowers quickly re-loading and firing again. His shots hit home and burst heads apart as Dave spins about killing anything that moves. Cookey joins him, then Lani and more until we're back together.

'Which way Lani?'

'Downhill please...' Nick begs.

'We need that road,' she points to a junction off to the left and we start moving that way. Forming into a small circle we lash out as the horde keep charging at us. Blowers, Cookey and Nick use their shotguns for several minutes but even in the dark I can see there are still plenty of undead left.

We keep moving and pick the pace up to try and stop them getting round behind us. They charge forward but their attacks are sporadic instead of concerted. Still we keep on as the church burns brightly behind them, flames licking out of the windows. They start to get co-ordinated and several attack at once. But with experience on our side we hack them down with our axes. Swinging out and gouging deep into their flesh. Killing with every few steps we take.

Reaching the junction we start moving downhill but that just gives them momentum in their charges and I can feel the weight of their bodies with every strike I make with my axe. My arms are burning and my legs shake and weaken with every step. I can sense everyone is feeling the same and the only thing that keeps us going is the fear of letting each other down. That and the bloody minded stubbornness of refusing to roll over and die quietly. They race past us and start trying to lunge in at the sides but for every desperate zombie face that tries to gnash and bite there is a dead zombie falling to the ground with its head cleaved open.

Grunts of effort emanate from behind me and then I realise that I'm doing it too. Making noises like a tennis player going for an ace serve. Looking across I see even Dave is starting to look tired and his normally pale face is flushed red which just makes him look angrier than normal. Clarence stumbles from a powerful swing and almost staggers out from our tight circle. Undead rush him but Dave springs out and slices them down as the big man rights himself and falls back into the round.

'That's for stepping on your head,' Dave shouts and even his voice sounds hoarse. Clarence doesn't reply but focusses on the same thing we all are. Staying alive and keeping motion.

We battle all the way down that bloody street. Leaving a trail of broken and mangled bodies in our wake but still they come. Darren must have pulled them from the church and kept them safe. Safe and waiting for us so he can grind us into the ground. But he doesn't do that. For some miraculous reason our strategy works, using axes and shotguns we've stayed alive and even if we die now we've killed hundreds and hundreds of them again.

'Sun,' someone croaks and I realise it's now much lighter than before. The only hope we've got of surviving is if they drop back when the sun comes up but Darren must see how exhausted we are. That we're ready to drop. The sky lightens as we head further down the hill, closer and closer to the beach and pier. They drop back, keeping pace but holding off from attacking and I can sense a change coming. We increase our speed not knowing where we're going or why we're going faster but it gives us a sense of purpose and something to aim for. More undead gather into their front ranks and we realise they're massing for a final attack. Preparing themselves for an offensive manoeuvre intended to finish us off.

There, further up the hill I see Darren and that woman, pacing a safe distance behind their zombies and holding them off until greater numbers can stagger forward and join their horde.

Dave and I both see him. We see that thing that has created all this death. Shotgun blasts sound out as the lads take advantage of the pause to get a few shots in. They do good work and whittle a few down. Cookey presses his pistol into Dave's hands and the small man fires one handed getting a head shot nearly every time. He passes it back and another one is handed to him, he fires again, dropping more and suddenly their numbers are reducing.

'Go into them,' I roar and change direction. We start pacing forward letting Dave fire pistols and taking the advantage away from them. Shotguns blast and the pistol fires. They die in numbers they can't afford to lose. The last remaining energy in my body surges into my muscles and we press home the attack. Darren realises we're killing too many and he sends them in. One final battle and we fight. We fight hard. Our power is low and every strike or swing hurts more than anything ever imaginable but we stay on our feet and swing out with everything we've got. Clarence stumbles again and drops his axe, they charge but he raises his fists and starts punching out keeping them at bay. One of Dave's knives leaves his wet hand stuck in the skull of a falling zombie but he presses on with one last blunt knife until it becomes nothing more than a useless tool and like Clarence he ditches it and takes to using his bare hands.

My axe flies back and forth, lifting high and slamming down but I feel weaker with every second. Another swing but it gets caught mid-air in the strong grip of a female zombie, still fresh looking with hardly any decay on her yet. She pulls the axe clean from my hands and I draw my pistol and fire point blank into her face. She drops down and I pick my shots, taking time to hit the skull. I have to keep stepping to avoid being taken. My pistol clicks empty and I start using it to hammer into their faces. I punch and gouge and writhe like a bastard to avoid their dirty teeth. My knee rises again and again into stomachs and groins, lashing out in a filthy street brawl. I start to get overwhelmed until Lani lashes out with her meat cleaver, driving them down and saving my life. I see a house brick nearby and pick it up. It becomes my new weapon as I slam it into the face of anything that comes at me.

Circling round I see my axe nearby and run to scoop it up, throwing the house brick hard at the head of a zombie about to bite into Blowers. Axe in hand I carry on swinging round as a glorious broad stripe of orange sunlight hits the pavement. The rays shine through the gaps in the buildings. Darren starts to lose control as some of them instantly slow to become the shambling daytime idiots. Others keep going but the fight is over. We know it and so does Darren. For the last few

minutes we kill off the remaining zombies in a blur of tiredness that staggers me to the core.
'FALL BACK,' Dave's hoarse voice yells and we start retreating. Letting the last few come at us instead of wasting our energy. Forming our circle we retreat. Stumbling like the daytime zombies now shuffling slowly after us. Lani leads us down a side street and then back down the hill. They keep coming but only one at a time now and they're easy to finish off. As we turn to start moving down the hill two figures stand at the far end of the street. Darren and Marcy stand amongst their ruined horde and stare quietly as we back away.
On seeing them I stop moving and stand still, staring back with my axe held down at my side. The others join me, spread in a line and staring back at the two figures. No one moves. They neither come forward nor retreat but stand watching us silently.
'I want to go after them but I've nothing left,' my voice is low and rough, barely more than a whisper.
'They'll run and none of us have the energy to chase them,' Dave replies but I watch his hands slowly pulling a pistol from his waistband. He ejects the magazine and quickly glances down to see it's empty. 'I need a bullet,' he whispers, 'just one.'
'Here,' Blowers slowly digs one out from his pocket and passes it along the chain, hand to hand until it reaches Dave, 'I was saving it for him.' Dave gently

slots the bullet into the top of the magazine and pushes it up into the pistol. He slides the top back and chambers the round. He stands with the pistol lowered and looks at the two zombies standing at the far end of the street. The distance is huge for a pistol shot. He holds still for a second before looking up into the sky and turns his head. His fingers flex on the pistol grip.
'Which one?' He asks.
'Do you need to ask,' I reply. He takes a deep breath and slowly exhales then moving with incredible speed he raises the pistol and fires.

 A solitary retort sounds out followed a split second later by one of the figures falling to the floor.

Chapter Sixteen

The day is going to be hot again. The air is listless without the slightest breeze. My rate of breathing has slowed and my heart gradually eases from the frantic work it's had to do all night.

There is blood on my hands and all down the front of my clothes. Sticky and moist. I can feel the wet material clinging to my skin.

Here in this quiet suburban street on the Isle of Wight I look back at the long line of corpses littering the road. At the top of the hill the church blazes fiercely. Thick smoke coiling up high into the blue sky.

'That was a good shot.'

'It was.'

'I can't feel my legs.'

'Your spine is broken.'

'So this is it.'

'Yes.'

'Do you want me to say sorry and beg for forgiveness?'

'No.'

'What do you want?'

'Nothing.'

'Then why are you watching me?'

'Waiting for you to die.'

'I might not die.'

'You're bleeding out.'

'Am I...oh shit.'

'Even you can't lose that much blood.'
'It doesn't hurt.'
'That's a pity.'
'She'll come after you…'
'I don't care.'
'I told her to go after you…she won't stop…she's better than me, stronger, clever, cunning…'
'I don't care.'
'You can't win this Howie.'
'Neither can you.'
'She's got my blood and everyone she bites will have my blood.'
'I don't care…they'll die just like you are now.'
'I'm tired.'
'You're dying.'
'Feel so….tired now…'
'Die then.'
'…I'm scared…I…'
'Die quietly.'
'Howie….please…'
'What Darren? What do you want?'
'Oh god I don't want to go like this…'
'Close your eyes Darren. Let it take you.'
'No…please…'
'Let it happen…'
'I'm so sorry…I'm sorry Howie…oh god I'm so sorry.'
'Me too Darren.'
'Forgive me…please…'
'No.'

'Please…I…oh shit…I'm going…'
'Darren…'
'Howie…please…'
'I forgive you Darren, rest now and let it take you.'
'Shit…oh shit…I'm bleeding…Howie…'
'Yes Darren.'
'H…Ho…Howie…'
'Yes?'
'Fuck you Howie…'
He dies with a smile on his face and just to be sure he dies fully and properly, Dave drops down and detaches his head with an axe and kicks it down the road. Marcy disappeared as soon as we started walking back towards them and with so much death and destruction it'll be near impossible to track her. I know because I asked Dave and Clarence.
I feel numb and strangely flat, like I was expecting a fanfare or some divine light to shine down when we finally got him but nothing happened. We stood in a filthy street and watched a former friend die. Now, standing round the body I can feel a deep sense of sadness that any of this had to happen.
'That was a good shot Dave,' I say just to break the oppressive silence.
'I was aiming for the head.'
'What from that distance?'
'I'm tired so I missed.'
'Bloody hell Dave you still got him.'
'Yes Mr Howie.'

'I'm bloody starving,' Nick interrupts rubbing his stomach, 'and I still want that swim.'
'Let's go down the hill then, we'll find some more clothes and food, have a swim and then find somewhere to sleep. Sound good?'
'Fuck yes please!' Cookey replies.
'Tom, you alright mate?'
'I'm fine Mr Howie.'
'You did well mate…sorry about Steven.'
'Thanks,' he nods back but his face remains expressionless.
'Lani, you too, you did well.'
'Cheers,' she smiles once, bright and gorgeous, 'can we go please, I'm hungry too and I desperately need to wash.'
'Yep, fair one.'

Chapter Seventeen

We head down through the deserted town centre. Walking slowly in the beautiful morning. No one speaks. All are absorbed in their own thoughts and utterly exhausted. I wonder if Tom and Lani would have come if they had known just how bad it would get.

She takes us to a cheap clothes shop with the windows already smashed in and we each grab clean tops, underwear, socks and a mixture of jeans and cargo trousers. Lani grabs a bikini from the shelf and makes it known that she will not be swimming in her underwear and that if anyone tries to swim naked she will shoot them.

'Does that include Blowers?' Cookey asks, 'seeing as he likes boys and not girls.'

'Cookey fuck off,' Blowers retorts with a shake of his head.

In a café we find tins of baked beans with mini pork sausages in them. Our hands are washed and scrubbed in the kitchen, using copious amounts of detergent to rinse the filth off. Eating straight from the tins with our axes stuffed down our bags we stroll down the hill, throwing the empty tins straight onto the ground and using the single tin opener we found to open more and stuff the contents into our mouths as quickly as possible. Reaching the esplanade we stare down the road at the blackened still smouldering buildings.

Finally on the beach we ditch our kit and start stripping off, the mood lifts slowly with idle banter being thrown back and forth. Lani makes Clarence stand with his back to her and holding a huge towel she got from the shop, she ducks round and changes into her bikini telling Clarence to make sure no one tries to sneak a peek. He stands like a protective bear glaring at the lads laughing and daring him to have a quick look. They fall silent when she steps out. We all do. The violent toughened zombie killer stands looking demure and breath-taking in her simple black bikini. I have to look away and busy myself with undoing my boot laces otherwise I would happily sit there gawping all day.

'That shut you up,' she laughs, 'so is a girl going to be the first into the sea,' she starts running as the lads shout that they're not ready yet. Ditching clothes as they run, they sprint down the beach and into the water, leaving me Dave and Clarence wondering where they got the energy from.

'Dave, you not coming in?' I ask as he stands there still dressed.

'I don't like the water,' he shakes his head, 'I'll keep watch here.' Clarence and I stroll down slowly. Enjoying the already warm sun on our bare torsos. The water is cool and refreshing, sending shivers through our tired bodies. The laughing eases as each person relaxes and lets the salt water cleanse them. Ducking heads under and rubbing our hair,

faces and bodies to rid them of the encrusted dirt. Lani swims over to me as I float on my back my arms and legs making occasional small movements to keep me afloat.
'I'm guessing we'll need somewhere to rest for a few hours,' she asks.
'Yeah, the pier looks good,' I nod towards the long black structure stretching out into the water just a short distance away.
'Okay…' her voice trails off suddenly hesitant.
'What's up?'
'Is it okay to come with you?' she asks quietly.
'Bloody hell Lani,' I laugh gently, 'I just assumed you would be, of course you should come.'
'I didn't want to just think it was okay.'
'You're one of us now Lani, a hardened killer of zombies…one of the elite,' I laugh again and she smiles back, a huge grin that suddenly makes me nervous again.
'Thanks for last night,' she says.
'Eh?'
'When you poured water on my face and made me rest, thanks for that.'
'Oh no worries…er…yeah…no problem…anytime.'
'Are you okay?'
'Yeah fine…should probably get out now,' I sink down and come up treading water and blinking the sea from my eyes.
'Mr Howie you get funny sometimes when you talk to me.'

'Do I? I didn't notice…' She smiles again and I curse myself for feeling the blush starting in my cheeks. She notices and laughs with delight and a sudden realisation.
'Don't laugh,' I groan.
'You're blushing…its sweet.'
'I'm not blushing…it's the sun.'
'Oh okay Mr Howie,' she laughs again.
'It's just Howie.'
'Everyone calls you Mr Howie.'
'I know right…bloody Dave started that off.'
'I can't call you Howie; it'll be weird in front of the others.'
'Well just when we're alone then.'
'Alone?' She raises her eyebrows and smiles as my cheeks burn from the even deeper blush I can feel spreading across my face.
'Ah bollocks you know what I meant, stop teasing me.'
'You alright boss your face is very red,' Clarence says as he swims over.
'Er…yeah it's the sun and I'm…er…knackered…time to get out I think.' As I swim away the surreal nature of it all hits me again. Tiny nuances of conversation, slight inflections of voice, a raised eyebrow, it's all part of our confused existence. Give me zombies to kill any day, Dave's got it right. Ignore anything that you don't understand.
A few minutes later we're all dressed in clean clothes and leaving our filthy garments in a pile on

the sand. Lani leads us from the beach having made Clarence hold the towel out for her again and I'm grateful that she's out of that bikini and into normal clothes. We start walking up the long pier, the lads joking around for the first few minutes until the tiredness creeps back in and we walk in silence.

At the end Lani leads us through the ferry terminal buildings to a café with one huge glass wall giving an amazing view of the bay and the town, and better still we can see the length of the pier. I split the group up and we search the buildings and rooms before gathering back in the warm room, Blowers and Cookey return with armfuls of big heavy winter coats used by the ferry and pier staff. Heavy benches are stacked against the double doors and we finally start settling down. Dave offers to take the first watch and promises to wake me after an hour.

 Too tired to protest I rest my head on my back pack and stretch my weary limbs out, resting on one of the big jackets. A backpack drops down near to my head followed by Lani kneeling down to smooth out a couple of jackets. There's plenty of space here and I wonder for a brief second why she's chosen to lie down so close. My eyes start to droop as I ponder the need people have for closeness and contact. A lone female amongst a group of men she barely knows, terrified and having lost everyone she knew in a world that's changed and become instantly dangerous. No wonder she wants to be near someone. Someone she senses she can trust.

As my eyes close and sleep starts to pull me under I feel a small hand touching mine. I open my palm and our fingers entwine. Gripping hard for a second I squeeze back, letting her know it will be okay.

Then I'm gone.

RR Haywood

Printed in Great Britain
by Amazon.co.uk, Ltd.,
Marston Gate.